Blood upon the Rose

Blood upon the Rose

Paul deParrie

CROSSWAY BOOKS • WHEATON, ILLINOIS
A DIVISION OF GOOD NEWS PUBLISHERS

Library of Congress Cataloging-in-Publication Data
Paul de Parrie
   Blood upon the rose / Paul de Parrie.
      p.   cm.
    I. Title.
PS3554.E5927B56 1992 813'.54—dc20   91-29818
ISBN 0-89107-639-5

00		99		98		97		96		95		94		93		92
15	14	13	12	11	10	9	8	7	6	5	4	3	2	1

*Dedicated
to Joseph Foreman,
a Presbyterian the way
they were meant
to be.*

ACKNOWLEDGMENTS

I would like to thank Dr. Herbert L. Baker for taking the time to clarify medical information for this work.

I appreciate the candid critiques of Mettie Williams in reviewing the early version of this manuscript.

Jan Dennis, who kindly agreed to read the story in his "spare" time, was of invaluable assistance in solidifying the characters and the tempo of the tale.

The editors and artists at Crossway who sweated over this project to make it come alive deserve my thanks.

Last and most important, thanks to my wife Bonnie, who will let nary a participle dangle nor a case be misplaced and did her best to ride herd on my grammar and syntax.

1

Large hands fitted the socket over the hexagonal nut and began to bear weight on the tight fastener holding down the car's starter. The space was cramped for the task of removing the stubborn unit from beneath the old Dodge van.

Jason Crabb lay on the creeper, straining against the ratchet handle, when it suddenly stripped past the nut, and his knuckles slammed against the vehicle's frame.

"Ow-w, sh . . . ," he said without finishing the word. Dropping the tool, he grabbed hold of his barked knuckles with the other greasy paw and scooted the creeper from under the van. Beneath his breath he uttered profuse apologies to God for his errant tongue. Holding one bleeding paw in the other, he shouldered the door open that led from the large, three-car garage to the utility room of the house. Beside the washer and dryer was a door to the small bath and shower he used before entering the tightly-organized house his wife Daniella ruled.

Jason Crabb was a large, burly man of thirty-eight years. He approached six feet tall, but fell a little short, and carried the extra baggage about his waist—testimony to Daniella's culinary abilities.

He slathered on the Goop grease remover and winced as it stung his mangled knuckles. "Gotta get the grease off to get at the wound," he reminded himself through gritted teeth. "This is what comes from overwork. You get tired— and you screw up," he chided himself. Jason had pushed himself on this van to get it ready for a quicker sale—but he now realized that the extra push was a mistake.

With his hands finally more or less grease-free, Jason doffed his work clothes, dumped them into the special hamper his wife insisted he use, and started the shower. The hot water running down his back seemed to drain the weariness out of him. He'd been standing under the stream for what seemed like ages when he heard Daniella call, "Jason! Jason, are you going to the hospital tonight?"

He stuck his head out into the steamy bathroom. "Ah, no, Hon. That's tomorrow night."

"I've been doing that all day for some reason," she replied. "I keep thinking it's tomorrow. I kept trying to give the kids the wrong school lessons. Well, dinner's ready in about fifteen minutes."

"What're we havin' anyway?"

"Having, not havin'—remember the kids. I've made a rice pilaf to go with the roast," she replied.

Moments later, Jason entered the living room and planted himself in the overstuffed chair in the corner. Just then seven-year-old Richard dashed into the room laughing maniacally with Monica, a five-year-old carbon copy of Daniella, squealing in his wake.

"Hold it," Jason held up the palm of his hand.

"But Richie—"

"But Richie, nothing, Monica. Neither of you should be

running in the house, and you know it. Go clean up for dinner, and we'll discuss this when you're done."

The two headed for the bathroom as three-year-old Nicole toddled in. She had an insatiable attachment for an old purse of Daniella's which she dragged behind her. "Daddy," she said and climbed up into his lap.

"How's Nicole?" Jason inquired.

"The baby is sleeping in your bed," she informed Jason, characteristically oblivious to his question.

The baby was James—a recent addition to the Crabb family by adoption. Daniella had been pleased with the idea, and Jason loved having babies around, so it seemed a natural step to take when they heard about this unwanted child.

At thirty, Daniella hardly looked old enough to be the mother of the youngest—much less Richard. She was very small, and dark brown curls fell down to the middle of her back. She looked out from hazel eyes and spoke quietly and evenly, communicating instantly a certain strength of character.

A clatter came from the kitchen, followed by Daniella's voice. "I forgot to tell you, Jason. Alvin Toley called. He had some questions for you about the case. He said to expect the papers on the lawsuit in the mail. They came today, and they are on your side table."

Jason picked up the thick manila envelope addressed from "Alvin Toley, Attorney at Law" and pulled out the weighty stack labeled "Complaint."

"Jason Crabb." His name was in the beginning of a short list on the left-hand side of the first page of a sheaf of papers. It was notice of a racketeering or RICO suit demanding over $27 million in damages. He, along with others, were charged as co-conspirators in a series of "crimes." All the local ringleaders were named—a sort of Who's Who of Oregon Pro-lifers. But Jason was no ringleader. Sure, he had carried a picket sign from time to time and even tried to sidewalk counsel, but his low-key nature kept him from any success there. He had written a letter or two to the editor. And he had joined in a rescue mission—well, actually, he was only there to pray, and he stayed on the sidewalk, but the police hauled him off for trespassing anyway. He was found guilty though he had never intentionally risked arrest. Now here he was, listed among the local pro-life stars.

The only reason he had attended the rescue in the first place was because he had been inspired by reading about a rescuer/psychologist named Bud Tower who had been railroaded on a phony assault charge and sentenced to five years in prison. The tale had gripped Jason's imagination— but not enough to compel him to block the doors. His reluctance, however, had not saved him from this lawsuit. Jason wondered if God was just trying to move him *toward* more activism or *away* from it. *Maybe I don't really believe that babies are dying. Maybe if I actually saw one dying. . .* , his thought trailed off.

Jason put the RICO papers down.

•

A wail broke through the early morning silence of the hospital delivery area. It was not enough to reach the ears of the child's father who was furiously engaged in the American Father's Smoking Ritual in the waiting area. Mother was virtually insensate—having requested "whatever medications are available" because of the difficult birth. Both had the utmost confidence in medical progress and shunned anachronistic home deliveries or natural births.

The nurse and the doctor exchanged glances, and the child—a seven-pound, ten-ounce boy—was bundled quickly off to the incubators in the room next to the nursery. The doctor would get someone to examine the child more closely after attending to the mother. The priorities were always straight at St. Luke's Hospital in Salem, Oregon.

"Take it easy, Pat," the trim, salt-and-pepper-haired ob/gyn said to the reclining patient.

•

He had no name—but that hardly mattered. The last few hours had been traumatic. His home had hugged him for some time, but the hugs grew tighter and pushed him head downward. It seemed he was being squeezed through a tiny tunnel, and the going was almost unbearable. After months of bouncing around in free-fall liquid, listening to voices and music and thumping heartbeats, he was surprised by the intensity of the experience.

Suddenly, there was light—brilliant, unremitting light—and he gasped. Gasped!? He breathed! He breathed, and it was not warm liquid. With a shock he expelled the foreign stuff, and with it came a loud sound that startled him.

There were no walls in this place—and he could no longer swim. He felt cool things that seemed to clasp parts of his body and move him about. Hard objects were thrust into his nose and mouth, rough sensations rubbed all over his body. Mumbling voices, like those he heard in the womb only louder and without the soft edges, surrounded him. What was happening?

He cried piteously—but he didn't know it was crying.

After a time, a strange warm thing was bundled around his body, and he was carried someplace and left to lay helplessly. The light was dimmer, but he was still in alien territory. The thing next to his skin in no way resembled his home—it was dry and rough.

Another new sensation was beginning—another unlike any before. There was a yearning that seemed located inside his belly. He smacked his lips in anticipation of . . . in anticipation of what? This subtle discomfort grew slowly but relentlessly, and soon he began again emitting sounds. Again things clasped his body, and he twisted his head seeking to close his mouth around the things.

Again the voices murmured, and again hard things prodded and poked at him. Where was his home? Where was the high voice that had often crooned in his hearing? He expelled air again and let out yet another long, startling sound.

•

Another kind of wail filled the garage where Jason Crabb worked busily under the Dodge van the day after his knuckle-busting feat. It was the wail of the slide guitar accompanying Patsy Cline's rendition of Willie Nelson's old '50s song, "Crazy." *This 318's in pretty good shape now,* he thought as he hummed along. *Now I just need to get Tom to squirt a coat of paint on this thing, and we'll be in business.*

Jason scooted out from beneath the van, fired up the motor, and listened intently. He grabbed his stethoscope and touched the probe to several places. Tilting his head, he focused on the internal engine sounds while mentally blanking out the music playing behind the hum of the motor.

Cutting off the engine, he picked up the phone and punched a single memory button linking him with Tom.

"Hey, Tom, I've got the Dodge van ready to go. Can I bring it over? . . . OK, I'll come later this afternoon. When will you be able to get this done?" He paused. "Sounds good to me. I'll see you then," he said and replaced the grease-stained phone on the hook.

His home business of buying, rebuilding, and selling older model cars generally brought in enough to support his burgeoning family, but the money was off and on. He owned the empty lot next to his home and usually had two or three cars out there ready for sale. He had a reputation for good work and reliability.

Again, Jason noted his chewed-up knuckles and shook his head. He looked out the window in the back of the garage and noticed Richard up in the vine maple. He seemed to have his eyes affixed on the nothingness of the blue sky above. "Always the dreamer," Jason said to himself, smiling inwardly at the memory of his own childhood spent in fantasy land.

For a long time, Jason just watched his son lost in childhood reverie. He imagined a painting or sculpture of the scene and wished he had an artistic flair. He had learned a lot about great art and literature from Daniella, but it did not come naturally to him as it did to her. Jason often listened with pleasure to Daniella's symphonies and sonatas, but his instinct locked in on other musical types.

"Daddy?" Monica's voice broke the spell. "Daddy, can we watch something on the VCR tonight?"

"Hm-m," Jason considered. "You'll have to ask Mom

about that, little one. Dad's going to the hospital tonight, so I won't be here to watch—it's up to your Mom."

•

Hours later, Pat Kelly sat upright in bed in a weary state of recovery. Beside her bed on the molded orange plastic chair sat her husband, Robert, looking disheveled.

With his hands in his lab coat pockets, Doctor Trumbill entered the room followed by a nurse.

"Doc," Robert said sounding relieved, "where's the baby? I went to look in the nursery, and he's not there yet."

Ignoring the question, Dr. Trumbill looked at Pat. "Are you feeling OK? Are you up to a visit from me?" The question elicited her nod, and he turned his attention to Robert. "That's what I'm here to talk to you about—the baby. I haven't had the specialist in yet, but the staff pediatrician confirms my suspicion of Down's syndrome."

"Down's syndrome?!" cried Pat sitting bolt upright. "You mean mongoloid?"

"Well, we don't call it that any more—but, yes."

"But . . . but what about the tests?" she implored. "They didn't show this. If we'd known, we would have taken care of it back then."

"I realize that, Pat, but none of these tests are 100 percent accurate. There's always a margin of error."

Pat folded her arms looking more angry than dismayed. "Well, what are we going to do *now*? What can be done?"

The doctor creased his brow and walked to the foot of the bed. He leaned against the footboard and said, "There is nothing that can be done about the baby's Down's—there is no treatment. It's genetic and permanent. But raising a Down's child is difficult and sometimes expensive."

"Raising?" Pat responded. "Raising? Robert and I have put off having children, and we *planned* this baby—planned right down to the nursery and everything. We didn't *plan* to have a retarded baby—and we're not prepared for it either." Tears began to well up in her eyes, tears not of sorrow, but of frustration and anger.

Robert broke in, "What are our options?"

"Really can't say until the baby has had its full exam," Trumbill said looking at the sandy-haired young father. "There could be other problems with it that haven't shown up—some of those problems could take the decision out of our hands completely."

"Meaning what?" Robert asked.

"Meaning that there are other problems that can—and often do—accompany Down's that are fatal in themselves."

Trumbill hesitated, seeing the confusion on Robert's face and the growing bitterness on Pat's. He added carefully, "Then there are those who opt to adopt their babies out in these cases."

"Adoption? Adopt out *our* baby?" Pat asked in a way that almost indicated protectiveness. But then her voice changed as she added, "Who would want a mongoloid, anyway?"

The nurse, who had unobtrusively hovered around Pat trying to attend to her comfort, injected, "Well, there are organizations that have lists of people who specifically want to adopt Down's babies."

Pat looked into the nurse's eyes, and the nurse saw the flat look that told her such suggestions were entirely unwelcome. She said no more. The doctor, also ignoring the nurse's suggestion, continued to talk soothingly and finished by saying that it was really too early to make ultimate decisions until the final report was in for the exam.

The nurse exited the room ahead of Dr. Trumbill.

•

St. Luke's Hospital rose out of the hillside off Cascade Drive
in West Salem like something out of a Gothic novel. The old
stone work displayed the workmanship of an earlier time.
A formal garden colored the ovoid patch before the old
front door and circular drive. It was surprisingly well kept
in a day when gang-mowers and chain saws were basic gar-
dening tools. From the road below, the hospital was decep-
tively small. Trees hid the wings that extended behind the
original building. Local preservation groups were wisely
responsible for having saved those trees, and now the
beauty of the campus repaid their efforts.

In another sense though, St. Luke's was an anachronism.
It derived its Biblical name from a time when such things
were not considered a violation of the separation of church
and state. Some of the locals still muttered that the name
should be changed, but even to them, the place was still St.
Luke's.

But for all of this antiquity, St. Luke's enjoyed a reputation as a progressive hospital. It had most of the latest giz-
mos and even a notable physician who acted as
bioethicist—real "big league."

Approaching the institution was a rather loud and
obnoxious vehicle that at one time could have been mistaken for a car. It was a typical mechanic's car—one that
never got worked on because the mechanic was too busy
working on other people's cars. The mechanic inside was
Jason Crabb. He whistled along with his taped western
music, oblivious to the car's rattles and shakes. Jason's
grandfather had left him a mint collection of platters of *real*
western music, as Jason described it. Not that sodden, sick
country-western stuff, but artists like Gene Autrey, Riders

of the Purple Sage, the old Hank Williams, and Patsy Cline. Wisely, Jason had the recordings professionally transferred to tape and had tucked the original disks and their jackets away. He delighted in turning down substantial offers for their purchase. Daniella preferred the classics—as she did with her reading, so Jason mostly listened while in his old car or working in the garage.

Spotting an empty space, he pulled in and turned off the ignition. The whole frame of the automobile shuddered its relief.

"Made it," he said to no one at all. He lifted on the door as he closed it and set off for the maternity wing—one of the new ones out back. Jason was here for his favorite ministry—cuddling babies. The program had begun some years back when the crack cocaine epidemic left the hospital awash with ever-crying, drug-addicted newborns whose mothers just disappeared. He comforted the little tykes as they faced the unexpected horrors of withdrawal symptoms—and it freed the staff from some of this additional work. He came once a week to hold "the littles," as he called them.

Jason walked across the grassy area beside the old building accompanied by the kre-e-et-kre-e-et of the night-singing crickets. The early summer's eve was warm and clear, and through the trees a small splattering of stars showed. He made his way to the side entrance and jogged up the steps to the intensive care nursery on the second floor. Observing hospital regulations, Jason donned a sterile gown. Then he reached up on a locker shelf for a large plastic squeeze bottle of hand lotion and applied a dollop to his rough hands—mechanic's hands.

The duty nurses always noted Jason with humor. Here was this rather large individual, with the hacked-up, permanently oil-stained hands that resembled greasy bear paws, carefully softening his skin so as not to scratch the tiny baby. Jason called it "industrial strength hand lotion."

"Hi, Jase," the nurse at the monitors' station said as he rubbed his lotion-soaked hands together.

"Hi ya, Terri," he grinned. "How're the littles? Any new-comers?"

"Yeah, a new girl over in the far corner there. But Bob Hines beat you to her. He got here fifteen minutes ago. You're next, though. All the other cuddlers seem to be late."

"The more for me," he replied smiling and headed toward the roomful of babies.

Over an hour passed before Jason emerged again, and when he did he nearly knocked Barbara Wiley to the floor. "Sorry," he said placing his hand on her shoulder. "You all right?"

Barbara was a small woman, only recently become a nurse. Her blonde hair was cropped short for work, but it did not properly frame her face—it made her jaws look heavy and unattractive. Still, she hadn't become a nurse for the social life. "It's OK," she replied. "I'm just a little dis-tracted."

To her, Jason was a comfortable figure. She had met him her first night in maternity and had come to regard him as a friend. "Well, Barbara," he answered, "you need to stop for a minute. Can you take a break? I'll buy you a cup, OK?"

"Sure, sure," she said. Her movements were jerky, and she kept darting glances down the hall. Jason could see there was a problem.

Together they walked down the dimly lit hall past the gurnies and laundry carts to the coffee urn. Jason put a cup under the spigot, pulled the lever, and allowed the dark brown liquid to fill the container.

"One lump or two?" he asked knowing full well she took it straight.

She reached for the cup and held it up to her lips with both hands as though trying to warm herself in winter. After a long draught, she put the cup down and said, "I guess it's none of my business after all."

"What?" he prodded.

"Yesterday a woman had a baby here that had Down's syndrome. She wasn't happy—the tests had shown nothing wrong. It was complicated with an esophagal atresia—a blockage in the throat that prevents swallowing. The procedure to clear up the atresia is pretty simple and safe, but the parents decided not to authorize it. It's their right to decide about their children's medical care—so now the baby is in the isolation room. I even told the mother about all the people who would adopt . . . I guess it's none of my business. I read about such cases in nursing school, and they say it happens all the time . . . "

"Well, what's being done to take care of the baby?" Jason asked with false calmness.

"We keep him clean and comfortable, but—but it doesn't seem right to me to let the baby die—especially from hunger and thirst. I mean, couldn't they just give it morphine or something? The doctor called it 'selective nontreatment.' But I guess it's not my business—it just bothers me, that's all. It was all theory in class; I guess I never expected to have to *see* it."

Jason was alarmed, but he dared not let her see how deeply. While many nurses were sympathetic to pro-life thinking, few would be willing to take positive action. Barbara was a product of her time—and a product of modern medical training. This meant that while she might object to the medical decisions, she would probably toe the line.

Jason tried to comfort Barbara, and soon he headed out to his car. Once out of view, he let his composure go. "Oh, Lord . . . ," he prayed, but had no more words. He climbed into his car and sat behind the wheel for a while mentally asking God what he should do.

He cranked over the motor, and it seemed reluctant to start up again. When it finally came to life, it had a hit-or-miss quality—mostly miss. But Jason's mind was not engaged by the sound of the engine. He did not, as formerly, promise himself to "do something soon about this old motor." But as he thought about the starving baby, an idea began to form.

"I'll need to talk to Daniella," he said out loud.

He wheeled on to highway 22, driving toward the bridge into downtown Salem. The thought of the starving baby clung to his mind. Almost too late, he saw the car from a merging lane cut closely in front of him. "You stupid little sh—" The scatological reference froze halfway out of his mouth. "There I go again, Lord," he said aloud. "Forgive me my filthy mouth and the uncontrolled mind that guides it. Boy, did James ever know what he was talking about when he said no man can tame the tongue!"

2

"Mr. Toley? This is Jason Crabb. I hate to bother you at home, but I have an emergency. You have a minute?"

Alvin Toley mentally readjusted his thinking from his Dave Brubeck music to the urgent voice in his ear. "Sure, no problem."

"I was up at the hospital tonight and . . . ," Jason began and launched into his tale. There was an occasional "Hm-m-m" and "Um-hm" from the attorney on the other end. "What I need to know," Jason concluded, "is what can I do about it?"

"Legally? Nothing, Jason," came the reply. "The courts in cases like these give complete authority for medical treatment to the parents."

"But that's just it—they aren't treating the little tyke," he replied.

"Back in the '70s, there was a very similar incident in Bloomington, Indiana—Infant Baby Doe, they called him. Pro-lifers tried to get an injunction to require the hospital to perform the medical procedure necessary to open the throat. But the courts said the pro-lifers had no 'standing' before the court," Toley explained.

"Standing?"

"That means that you are somehow involved directly in the issue before the court. For instance, if I saw someone injure you, I could not sue your assailant—only you or your family could. Only they would have 'standing.'"

"What if I offer to adopt the baby and pay all the medical bills? Wouldn't that give me this 'standing?'" Jason asked.

"Hold on, Jason. You sound as if you're ready to jump into this with both feet, and you really need to know the legal situation. Many people offered to adopt Infant Doe in Bloomington, but in the end, he was starved to death. The courts could not care less if someone wants to adopt and pay the bills. They stand on the 'principle' of parental rights—at least in this instance."

"Well," Jason said, "I suppose that even if it made a difference in court, the baby would be too far gone by the time anything could be done."

There was a silence from Toley's end of the line. Finally, he said, "Nothing can be legally done for the boy, and it would probably be too late if it could. I suppose all we can do is pray, Jason."

"Maybe—maybe not," Jason answered. "Thanks for your help, Mr. Toley. I appreciate you taking the time to answer my questions."

•

"There are actually three kinds of atresia," Dr. William Celcis said into the cradled phone receiver as he plucked the tea bag out of the mug and measured the sugar into the steaming brew. "What's this about, Jason?"

"First tell me how much is involved in fixing it—can you do it?"

"Well, with the two worst types it involves opening the chest to get at the esophagus—this is where the esophagus simply dead-ends or actually switches tracks and leads into the windpipe and lungs. The other type is a narrowing with too small an opening for food to pass. This can be corrected with dilatation—could do it in my office. Of course, at the hospital they have a laser that is faster and more efficient. . . ."

"What kind of follow-up would a newborn need after these?" Jason added anxiously.

"Just a watch for twenty-four hours against perforations for the last type. The others—well, we'd probably put in a gastrostomy, a tube in the stomach, to feed him if that were a problem," Celcis observed.

"How long can someone go with a gast—gas—stomach tube?"

Celcis sipped at his tea and placed the cup on the table in front of him. "If properly cared for—indefinitely. There are people who go to work every day who have gastrostomies. Now, what's this about?"

"Can't discuss it with you now, Bill. I'll probably see you at your office tomorrow and let you know then."

The rest of the conversation was primarily around fishing—a passion for both of them. But Celcis was still puzzled by the call. *Jason is just not the type to ask questions of that kind,* he thought. He picked up his tea—long since cold—and returned the cup to the kitchen sink.

•

Jason tried to study the RICO complaint. He was supposed to fill out the client questionnaire supplied by Toley so that the attorney would be able to represent the group better. But Jason's heart was back in a small, dark room at St. Luke's.

Jason looked at the papers, then at his wife. Daniella sat in the padded rocker, reading to the children from *Little House in the Big Woods* by Laura Ingalls Wilder. Richard stood behind the chair looking over her shoulder. Nicole had her forearms on the arm of the chair and was suspending herself. Monica sat on the floor, and the baby, James, adopted from the cuddler group, lay in Daniella's lap playing with his toes.

They were just winding up their evening chapter before bedtime—actually they were about an hour late for bed, but Daniella insisted they get their chapter in. Now they headed off to their beds.

"I've got to do *something*," Jason said to Daniella as she came back into the room with two glasses of lemonade. He had already told her the basic facts and, as yet, she had said nothing. "If I took the little to Celcis, I'm sure he would take care of the artes—, the atres—, well, you know, the blocked throat."

"What then, Hon?" Daniella asked.

"I don't know. I suppose he could stay with Doc for a few days—maybe we can find someone to take him in. Heck, maybe *we* could take him in."

"I wouldn't mind that, but remember the mother's reaction to Barbara's suggestion of adoption? I don't think they would change their minds. It sounds to me as if the parents are *embarrassed* for having an 'imperfect' child and want *no one* to know of it—they want to bury their 'mistake.'"

"Well, we can't just let him die, can we? The Word tells us to feed the hungry and not to just say, 'Be warmed and filled.'"

"The only resolution here," Daniella said, "is to pray first. John Bunyan once said, 'You cannot do more than pray until you have prayed.'"

That was one of the things that always amazed Jason about Daniella. She always had an appropriate word that was not a mere platitude. Jason nodded.

Both bowed their heads and began quietly to call upon God. After a time, they lapsed into silence. The stillness grew until they were both enveloped in God's presence. Jason opened his eyes and looked down at the open Bible on the coffee table. There, in the center of the page, a section seemed to jump off the page—it was the story of the Good Samaritan.

"I know what I must do," he whispered almost as though to himself. He set the RICO suit papers aside and went to the hall closet. Once there he pulled out an old lab coat he had used as part of his uniform when he had worked for a fast-lube place. He held the company name tag and began to cut the stitches to remove it.

•

Early morning light glowed on the eastern walls of St. Luke's. People bustled through the halls, but few were really aware of their surroundings.

Jason had been sitting in a dark corner of the parking lot for two hours trying to summon the courage to open his car door. *What am I doing here?* he asked himself for the thirty-seventh time. His stomach muscles knotted, and he felt he would vomit as he finally lunged for the door handle and popped open the door. The step to the pavement felt as if he were taking his first parachute jump. He pulled himself out of the car and began to walk stiffly toward the side entrance to the hospital.

The night shift had wearily trudged to their vehicles or the bus and gone on home to the comfort of their beds. The morning shift was frantically trying to align themselves with the changes that had occurred overnight—and trying to do it through propped-open eyes and muddled brains that waited for the first strains of caffeine to startle awake their brain cells. Jason counted on that as he walked inside. "Here we go," he muttered to himself.

Looking around and locating a recognizable landmark inside, Jason jammed his knuckle-busted scarred hands into the lab coat pockets and walked as casually as he could manage through the halls of the maternity ward. A name badge pinned to the coat hid the ragged spot where the lube company's name had been. Around his neck, Jason wore a stethoscope that he often used to troubleshoot automobile engines. *It's a nice touch,* he thought. He hoped no one would recognize him on this shift—especially through the prevailing madness.

He looked down the hall to the isolation room that Barbara Wiley had indicated with her anguished eyes. Boldly, he strode to the door and pulled the chart from the slot beside the door. The top sheet was emblazoned with a red sticker bearing the white letters, "DNR." He knew that it was a euphemistic death sentence, "Do Not Resuscitate," for the baby. Jason scanned the contents as though searching for something. Still looking at the sheaf of papers, he pushed open the door and disappeared inside.

There in an isolette cart lay the little boy. The lights were low, and there was nothing "plugged in" to the tiny figure— no IV, no nothing. The light seemed to startle the baby, and he began to quietly whimper.

The baby had a mass of brown hair and large, blue eyes. There was a hint—though not much—of the characteristics that gave the name "mongoloid" to his condition. His little arms waved in the air as though struggling with some unseen opponent.

Jason leaned against the inside door frame, his heart pounding as if demanding to leap out of his chest. His knees felt weak—and yet, the most dangerous part was yet to come. At the thought of it, new fear gripped him.

Forcing his fear under control, Jason stuck the papers into the carrier at the end of the isolette.

"It's all right, my little victim of circumstances," Jason said quietly as he picked up the bundle. "I'm gonna take care of you. There, now, I'll hold you for a bit—then we'll get outta here. Just a day and a half into this world and already in deep trouble, huh?" Jason was glad the child could not sense the anxiety he felt or know of his horrible desire to abandon the effort right there.

•

There was an unrelenting pain in his stomach, and he could do nothing but cry—at least until he was too tired to continue. By the time he woke, his mouth was so gummy and dry that even crying was impossible. He could not bring up the strength to even let out a yelp when the light suddenly brightened from time to time. Sometimes, things would handle him roughly, and that hot, stingy feeling would disappear from the middle of his body, but there was no comforter for him.

This time, when the light got bright again, he let out a low moan. This time, a sound seemed to answer, and someone picked him up and held him warmly. It was the closest thing to the secure feeling of his old home that he had had since—it seemed like forever. In fact he had almost entirely forgotten that snuggling warm, wet, bouncy feeling of home.

•

Shortly, Jason returned the struggling child to the container, changed his diaper, and stashed a handful of the disposable variety into a bag. *No one's gonna believe a real doctor is pushing this thing himself*, he thought. He felt a sense of panic, but quickly he formulated a new wrinkle in the plan. He stowed the stethoscope with the baby, piled a few old receiving blankets over the baby, and wheeled the isolette out the door and down the hall, hoping he would be taken for an orderly taking the isolette and the blankets for cleaning.

Just look purposeful, Jason thought to himself. *Just act like you know what you're doing—and pray the baby is quiet.*

Already Jason could see the caffeine-brightened eyes in a number of faces, but he looked directly at them and nodded, "Morning." Ahead lay a corridor that led to a side entrance near the staff parking lot where Jason had left his car. This was his goal. He sweated mentally and hoped no one would notice his hands—a dead giveaway that he did not work there.

Almost without a glance from any of the staff, Jason made it to the hallway and headed for the door. The green lettering of the "Exit" sign read "home" to Jason.

"Orderly!" a voice came from behind.

Jason turned slowly, hoping it would not be someone who knew him. "Yes," he said as he turned and faced the unfamiliar nurse.

"What are you doing?"

"I'm takin' this stuff, ah, I'm takin' it for cleaning."

"I asked for someone to do housecleaning in 113A."

Jason feared the child might stir, or worse, wake and cry out in its weak way. He had to detach himself from this situation—fast. "Uh, yeah, that's right," he said. "They told me to do that, but I'm supposed to finish this first. This'll only take about ten minutes, OK?"

"Well, all right," the nurse answered. "But I need that done fast. So be quick about it."

Quickly, Jason spun around and wheeled the cart out the door. He had gotten no more than a few feet when a low cry came from beneath the pile of receiving blankets, and they moved with the baby's kicks.

"C'mon with me, little victim," Jason said as he reached down and scooped the child from the carrier. He wrapped a couple of the clean receiving blankets around the tyke and opened the car door. One of the blankets had been placed across the chrome handle of the little gurney to prevent fingerprints. *Not a half-bad rescue plan for a mechanic*, Jason thought with satisfaction. *Now to see Doc Celcis.*

Jason still had the baby car seat from three-year-old Nicole in the trunk and had moved it to the front seat in anticipation of the rescue effort. He buckled down the little child. Beside the car seat, Jason tossed the baby's paperwork. It read: "Baby Boy Kelly."

●

It was Saturday, midmorning, and Dr. Celcis sat at his desk filling in some reports from his notes. There were no patients today—none that he had planned for, anyway. The clinic's location on Commercial Street put him near a lot of poor and desperate people who came as patients. But despite the background of traffic noises, things were relatively quiet at the clinic on weekends. With a start he became aware of the rattling car sounds invading the solitude of his office. They seemed to be right outside. In fact, they *were* right outside.

The doctor pulled down on the miniblinds and looked into his parking lot to see Jason's old—really old—Dodge. Jason was leaning into the passenger side retrieving something. *Probably one of his kids,* Doctor Celcis thought and headed toward the locked side door to the office.

When he swung wide the door, Jason stood facing him with his arms full of pastel receiving blankets and a wad of papers in one hand. "Doc, I *knew* you'd be here. I need your help—well, actually, *he* needs your help," he said nodding toward the blanket-bound bundle in his arms.

Before the doctor could open his mouth, Jason was off again. "Lissen, Doc, this kid's got that artesia—or whatever you call it—check it out on the paperwork. Anyway, they were gonna let him starve. The nurse who told me said they call it 'selective nontreatment'—how's that for a nice way of saying 'kill?' So, I figured maybe you can fix him up, and I can find him a home. What d'ya say, Doc?"

Celcis looked stunned. He began slowly, "If you took this baby from the hospital without permission—don't you realize that they'll call it kidnapping?"

"Hey, Doc," Jason said, "I know you are a believer and a strong pro-life doctor. I thought about it—I prayed about it. All I could think about was the Good Samaritan and how the religious bigwigs didn't feel like they were called to a 'ditch ministry'—yeah, a ditch ministry is what one guy in the pro-life movement called it. Anyway, look at this kid, will ya? I couldn't look God in the face at judgment if I knowingly let this guy starve—could *you*?"

The doctor was silent. Then he sat down at his desk, picked up the charts, and carefully examined them. After a nervous moment, Jason said, "Doc?"

The doctor held up his hand and continued to look over the papers. "Yes, you're right," he finally said. "They were going to 'nontreat' him to death—and for the simplest of atresias, too. This stuff makes me so angry," he added pointing to the papers. "I won't need to do anything drastic like a gastrostomy or open him up, thank God. But I will need to watch him for twenty-four hours after the dilatation."

"Dilatation?" Jason looked puzzled.

"The boy has a very small opening in his esophagus—too small for food. We need to use a series of dilators to make it wider, but I'll have to keep an eye out for a day for any punctures. The danger is relatively minor. I'll start right away—bring him back into the surgery."

"How can I help?" Jason asked.

Celcis looked at Jason's hands. "With those? Probably best if you start lining up some contacts. All of this is *very* illegal, and this baby will need to disappear—fast! You can use the phone in my office—first call Marlene. My wife has some nursing skills, and she'll assist me here. One of the advantages of living next door to your office."

With that, Celcis picked up the child and began to gently examine him. Jason headed toward the office.

3

The headline in the local section of the Sunday morning edition of *The Sun* read, "BABY MISSING FROM HOSPITAL, PARENTS FEAR FOUL PLAY." The story explained the disappearance of the baby and identified him as a "special-needs child" requiring "medical treatment."

"The paperwork was gone and the room left clean," said one hospital source. "So it was assumed that the baby had been moved somewhere else. But the baby needs treatment. I hope whoever took him will bring him back soon."

Reading the article only touched off Jason's concern for the little boy. *Treatment?* he thought acidly. *Treatment to death. If the people only knew. If the paper told the whole truth. . .*

It was still too early for church, and Richard and Monica were clearing the breakfast dishes. Daniella was kneeling bent over the edge of the bathtub washing little James.

"Hey, how are you, Jimbo?" Jason asked the squirming little body in the sudsy water. Then he turned his attention to his wife. "Lissen, Hon, I'm going to check on the little victim and maybe take him to the couple who promised to help us find him a home. I'll meet you at church if I can, OK?"

Daniella always managed to look as though even the worst circumstances and most strained situations were completely natural. Without even looking up she answered, "All right. See you there."

Jason bent down, kissed her cheek, and placed his hand on her shoulder for a moment as if to draw strength. He often did this when times were tough. It was her serenity that had first attracted him to her. She was not your typical twenty-one-year-old, and though he was eight years older than she, he saw a strength in her faith that he lacked. She had been raised in a believing home and had never departed from the teachings of her youth. He, on the other hand, had only walked with Christ for about five years before they met.

But this time when Jason touched her, he felt a sense of loss—or pain—or something inexplicable. He uttered a prayer under his breath, "Oh, Lord, be with us whatever way this goes."

Quickly he left the house, climbed into the old beater, and cranked up what was left of its engine. The Dodge rolled back out of the driveway and headed down the street toward Celcis's Commercial Street clinic. With him, Jason carried the local section of the paper with the missing baby story. He wanted to take it with him to Tim and Wanda Oberstraat's house if he took the baby there—he knew they rarely got the paper.

The sight of the clinic shifted his thoughts back to the little boy. *Little victim, so young and in so much trouble.*

The light was on in the office window, so Jason pulled up next to the side door. The door was unlocked and Jason entered and found Celcis sitting again at his desk. The doctor looked up through reddened eyes. "Oh, it's you," he said. "Marlene's got him next door—sprucing him up, I suppose. You'll find a bandage on him where I hooked him up to an IV to rehydrate him. You'd be surprised how dried out a little one can get in just a day or two. Otherwise, he's fine. We don't have a wet nurse, so I picked up some formula for him. He'll probably need some other stuff though."

"Other stuff?" Jason said. "Oh, no! I left it at home. Daniella put some baby stuff together in a bag for the little. I only live a mile away—I'll go get it and be right back to pick up the baby."

Jason got back in his car and drove off. He headed up Commercial Street where it joined River Road and on towards Bever Drive, just across the Salem city limits into Keizer, where he lived. As he approached his street, he saw two police cars pass through the intersection into Bever. He tensed and suddenly grew cautious. Nearing the intersection, he looked down Bever Drive. There in front of his house were half a dozen police cruisers—three from Keizer, two from Marion County, and another from Polk County. Whirling lights of red and blue gave a surreal look to the scene—Daniella, holding James and surrounded by the other children, talking to a police officer.

"Nabbed!" Jason said to himself as he continued past the intersection and rounded the block. "Better get back to Doc's and get the baby quick. No telling how much they know. Wonder how they found me out?" It was obvious what all the cops were about. Salem, Oregon, rests in two counties—Marion and Polk. West Salem, where St. Luke's was located, was in Polk, while the remainder of Salem— and all of Keizer—were in Marion County. The Polk Sheriff's Department was in touch with Marion County and Keizer's city cops as a matter of jurisdiction—and courtesy—on this bust.

●

"I really can't tell you where he is now," Daniella said hoping they wouldn't notice the scrupulous construction of her words. "He left a while ago. He said he would probably see me later. What's this all about?"

Two more squad cars were pulling up to the house as the Keizer police sergeant answered, "We need to question him about an incident at the hospital where he's been a volunteer."

Daniella looked up at the tall sergeant whose gray eyes gave no indication of his deceptive ploy to capture Jason, the suspected kidnapper.

"My," Daniella noted innocently but with the slightest tinge of irony, "so many police cars just to question one man."

The sergeant looked around nervously, composed himself, and answered, "Oh, the report to get hold of Mr. Crabb went out over the radio. I guess everyone just responded. This hospital incident has a high priority."

"Oh, I see," she replied.

●

Jason entered the doctor's house suddenly, and Marlene looked surprised. "The police are at my place," Jason said as he walked over to the baby. "I don't think they know about what you and Doc have done or they'd be here, but I've got to get the little out of here and get him lost—and maybe me too. Call my attorney, Alvin Toley, and tell him what's happened and to get his fingers on the pulse of this situation for me. Tell him I'll contact him later at his house. In fact, tell him all this anonymously so there's no connection to you and Doc. I never told you or Doc where I was taking the little, so there's no connection there. See you later—I hope."

With that Jason popped out the door with the baby in his arms. Marlene quickly scooped up a bag of baby things and followed him from the house and flung it on the floor of Jason's Dodge. "You'll need some of the stuff in here. There are diapers and some formula and a couple of bottles," she said.

Jason looked across at her and, for lack of anything else to say, stated, "I hate driving kids around in this old thing, but I guess I have no choice."

As Marlene disappeared into the house, Jason pulled out his wallet to check his funds. There was six hundred dollars in fresh twenties that he had picked up from the bank on Friday to pay for some engine parts he had ordered. Jason liked to pay cash to keep his books clear of credit. Fortunately, he had forgotten to pick up the parts in all the excitement. *Hmm*, he thought, *I've got a $300 draw limit on my bank card. Who knows if I'll need that much or not—but it's better to be safe. I'll pick up the $300.*

Then another thought occurred to Jason. *I'd better use a machine that's not near Doc's in case they trace the withdrawal. Probably better use one in the center of town—better yet, I'll use one near the I-5 freeway. Maybe they'll think I headed toward Portland.*

Jason piloted his car north on Commercial, turned onto the Salem Parkway, and drove toward its intersection with I-5. Near the intersection, he located a bank machine that would take his card and withdrew $300. Soon he was heading south on I-5. He planned to take the North Santiam Highway and find the home of the Oberstraats in the farming community of MacLeay southeast of Salem.

It was a short trip. The little community moved at a slow rural pace—especially on Sunday. Small independent churches had dotted the countryside as he passed through. There in the parking lots were the cars that would normally be on the road or parked "'round back of the house." Jason's noisy Dodge was conspicuous by its presence, and though he knew it was unlikely the MacLeay police would know of him yet, he felt as if malevolent unseen eyes watched his solitary use of the road.

He took a left off MacLeay Road onto 78th Avenue and quickly located the gray house with white trim. The Oberstraats weren't farmers. They had merely bought the place. Tim always used to joke that they had "bought the farm"—back before the Oregon land conservation laws prohibited cutting such farms up. They had cordoned off about ten acres for themselves and sold the rest of the farm to a real farmer. To the Oberstraats, this was their retirement home.

Over the years, Tim and Wanda had fixed the place up. On the outside, it looked like a well-kept farmhouse and barn—though some would say it was merely a large shed— but inside the house were all the latest conveniences. The house itself sat nearly at the gravelly end of 78th and well off the road. It could be missed easily as it sat among the trees.

Tim was a retired journalist with worldwide connections. He was also a ham radio enthusiast—which only extended his reach. A tall antenna stood out on the rise behind the copse of trees surrounding the house.

When Jason pulled around back of the house, he was instantly aware that the Oberstraats were not there. *Probably in church,* he thought. The baby was beginning to fuss, so he turned his attention to the child.

•

"So what's going on, Alvin?" Jason asked the lawyer over the phone as he sat in the hallway at the Oberstraats. From the living room, he could hear Wanda cooing over the little boy.

"Well, they are pretty tight-lipped, Jason," Alvin Toley replied. "I think they are going to charge you with abduction—pretty serious stuff—and if you leave the state, it will be a federal kidnapping charge."

"What kind of information do they have?"

Alvin was quiet for a moment, and then he answered, "It seems they were led to you by questioning the hospital staff. One of the nurses said she had told you of the little Kelly boy. Evidently, no one outside of staff and the parents knew—except you. And *you* are a known radical—at least to them."

"So how long am I going to need to dodge the cops?" Jason asked.

"There's no telling, Jason," Alvin answered. "It could be a long time. It depends on what you are willing to face up to in the way of charges."

Jason shot back, "As far as I'm concerned, it depends on what will happen to the little victim here."

"In either event, Jason, we must be prepared for the worst and plan for a long stay underground. I'll handle things on this end. As your lawyer, I have a certain level of confidentiality that no one else has. We need to set up communication rules."

"Yeah, I thought of that," Jason said. "I have an idea on how to make sure messages are really from each other. But first, how are Daniella and the kids doing?"

"You know Daniella, she's handling it well. I'm going to

set up a system to keep the bills paid over there, so don't be worried about that. It's a good thing the business is in her name; that way the state can't come in and impound everything."

Jason replied, "Well, Daniella was always the one who could handle business stuff—I'm just a mechanic. I guess it worked out as a blessing to do it that way."

The two continued to plan strategy for the next hour and a half—communications, movements, evasion techniques, and so on. By the time it was over, Jason had a pile of notes which would have to be organized into a small notebook to carry along if this adventure should stretch out over a long time. Finally, he emerged into the Oberstraats' living room to find the baby sleeping and Tim and Wanda talking quietly.

"I got things set up with my attorney, Alvin Toley—you know him, right?" Jason said softly.

Tim answered, "Sure. We know Alvin."

"Well, he'll be in touch with you. He says this could be a long haul," Jason added. "I would really like to pray with you folks about this situation and the little victim here. Y'know, I can't go on calling him 'the little victim' if we're to spend so much time together. We've gotta give him a name."

Wanda took Jason's hand and patted it. "We are going to pray that the baby comes out the winner in this. Why don't we call him Victor—to remind us of the victory in Jesus?"

"Sounds good to me," Tim said. Jason nodded.

"Then Victor it is," Wanda said. And they all joined hands to pray.

•

RACKETEER SOUGHT IN KIDNAPPING; SUSPECT ELUDES POLICE

Salem, OR—Police announced today that they are seeking an anti-abortion extremist, Jason Crabb, in connection with the abduction of a newborn baby from St. Luke's Hospital on Saturday. Crabb is a defendant charged with racketeering under federal RICO statutes.

Police officials say that Crabb is their prime suspect and is likely to be charged with felony abduction. Captain Blevins of the Marion County Sheriff's Department says that this crime could become a key incident in the racketeering charges against Crabb.

Hospital representatives and police are at a loss to explain why the thirty-eight-year-old part-time auto mechanic who sells used cars would kidnap the infant. "One thing that is important to say," Dr. Aaron Trumbill, who delivered the child, said, "is that the baby desperately needs medical treatment—and, in fact, will suffer needlessly without it."

Neither Daniella Crabb, the suspect's wife, nor Alvin Toley, his attorney, could be reached for comment.

The names of the parents of the child have not been released. "Understandably, they are very distressed," Trumbill said. "They were under quite a strain already with the child's medical problems—and all the attendant difficult decisions. Now they have had their child stolen. It is all very tragic."

Could not be reached for comment, Daniella thought as she scanned the article in the Monday edition of the *The Sun. They never even tried.* The references to Jason as a racketeer were particularly galling to her. *They've got him tried and convicted as some kind of gangster.*

Just then the phone rang. Daniella reached across to the end table and lifted the receiver. Alvin Toley's rich baritone voice came across clearly. "I suppose you've seen the paper?" he asked.

"Yes," she said.

"They are trying to use the RICO law to impale Jason in the public mind. The reporter who called me *did* get my comments, but he chose not to use them and made me look evasive. I told the guy why Jason had taken the baby—but that information didn't fit his prewritten story. The Portland TV stations covered the story straight from his wire report, so they had the same slant. Most of the reporters at *The Sun* would have run the stuff I said just for the conflict alone, but this is one of those reporters with an agenda," Alvin said.

"Is there anything we can do?" Daniella asked.

"As a matter of fact, there is, Daniella," Alvin said with apparent relish. "There are ways to bypass the press entirely, if need be. But I have some ideas that the press will not be able to ignore. This *Sun* reporter doesn't control the whole shebang, but he's hoping to vilify Jason and drum up sympathy for the parents early in the game. The hard part for us will be to overcome the sympathy for the grieving parents that the press will surely focus on."

"You mean we need to go public with the whole thing?" Daniella asked. "Won't that help the police find Jason?"

"Not if we play our cards right, Daniella. I've got a scheme working right now that may blow the lid off this little attempted child murder."

4

Victor opened his eyes. In his middle was a nagging, uncomfortable feeling called hunger. But it was nothing like the hunger he had once known—a hunger that had now almost completely faded from memory. Now he had warm holding and plentiful food and dry diapers.

He had begun to recognize a familiar sound—a low sound, not like the one he used to hear while he was in his now-forgotten watery home. This sound nearly always preceded warm holding and an end to his discomfort of hunger.

It wasn't happening fast enough at the moment though, so Victor let out a wail to bring it more quickly.

•

"When I was working in Kampuchea covering the refugees coming out of there, I got to know Mr. Nguyen—that's the Kampuchea equivalent of Smith, not his real name," Tim Oberstraat said. "He worked inside under Khmer Rouge noses providing false papers to get people out of the country. He finally got caught, but escaped and made his way across the border. He lives in Salem today—runs a print shop. I think he may be able to help us with some ID for you and Victor."

"Can he be trusted?" Jason asked.

"He's a brother in Christ, Jase, one that took me on a wild tour in Kampuchea and nearly got blown away by the Rouge to cover for me," Tim answered. "Yeah, he can be trusted."

"OK, what's your plan?"

Tim grabbed a sheet of paper and pen to illustrate his idea. "Look, we get you a new name, driver's license, birth certs for you and Victor. After that, we can pick up another car for cheap, fix it up, and you'll be a lot freer. No one will find that old Dodge of yours out in the barn and under a tarp. We need to change your appearance a bit though. How about a buzz cut?"

"A what?"

"A buzz cut—a real short haircut. Then grow a Van Dyke beard."

"I hate beards. Every time I have tried to grow a beard or mustache, it itches so bad that I cut it off. I don't mind the short haircut. My hair is always too long anyway, but a beard?"

Tim looked a little exasperated. "Look, you need to look different enough so you won't be easily spotted. Suppose you have to move on from here? You'll need to be convincingly different. Most clean-shaven fugitives attempt a beard as a disguise—a full beard, not a neatly-trimmed one. This will give you a photo for the driver's license that looks really different. A little itch is a small price to pay—only you'll have to learn not to scratch it and give yourself away."

"All right, I suppose I can do that," Jason answered resignedly. "So what name will we use?"

"I think we can get away with calling Victor by that name since his parents didn't give it to him, but we'll need to call you James—something close to your real name—and for a last name for you both, how about Cramer? James and Victor Cramer."

"OK," Jason replied. "But first we have to get all this hospital paperwork to Alvin. He has plans for it."

"I can take that stuff to him tomorrow. I'll see Nguyen the same day to get him working on the papers—he'll have to research the processes of local ID in order to get it done right. He's been out of the phony papers racket for quite a while. Meanwhile, you work on that beard for your photo, OK?"

"All right," Jason said rubbing the two-day stubble on his chin. *With my heavy beard, it shouldn't take long,* he thought.

•

The press conference had gone better than expected. Alvin escorted Daniella and her children out of the meeting room, through the throng of calling reporters, and into a waiting automobile. Saturday morning about ten o'clock was the slowest time for news gathering, and Alvin Toley knew it. The story would hit the wires and be covered by the noon and evening news. The starved Sunday editions of the paper and electronic media would carry it all of Sunday—and lazy editors would slip it in on the slow copy of Monday's edition. The story had a chance even to be picked up nationally.

The conference had been held in Portland to make it more likely that reporters would show. Now they would have just enough time to make it to Salem to catch the noon coverage. Toley already had video machines covering all the Saturday news channels for the record.

"I think we did real well, Daniella. And especially you kids—you will look great," Alvin chortled. "Showing the world what a normal family Jason has will make it hard for people to think of him as a criminal."

"Do you think those papers will help?" Daniella asked. "I couldn't make anything of them."

"Did you see the first page with the big DNR on it? That means, 'Do Not Resuscitate'—or, if something goes wrong for the person, let 'em die. The reporters will get all of that translated through their own sources, and it will work out to just what I told them—the parents were killing the baby by starvation."

"Where to, boss?" asked the driver. He was actually Alvin's legal secretary.

"You see how he pretends respect when we're in public?" Alvin quipped. "Swing by a McDonald's and get something for these kids. Then head home—fast."

The secretary shook the blonde hair from his eyes and said, "Righto, boss." Then he wheeled the new Mercury up Burnside to the McDonald's at 18th Avenue. After a trip through the drive-thru lane, they emerged with a carload of bags emblazoned with golden arches.

"This is not what I normally like to feed the kids," Daniella said seriously.

"Nor I," said Alvin, "but these are not normal times. And besides, these kids have done real well and still have another long, boring ride ahead. I figured they could use something with 'kidnip' in it as something special."

Daniella just shook her head and took a long draw from her soft drink.

•

The newscaster's face looked grave as he said, "And now a bizarre twist on that newborn kidnapping last week in Salem. Today the attorney for the alleged kidnapper and the wife and family of the fugitive held a press conference claiming that the child was abducted in order to save its life. The attorney, Alvin Toley, long noted for his flamboyant style in and out of the courtroom, produced copies of hospital documents from an undisclosed source, showing, he claimed, that the child was being denied simple life-saving treatment merely because it was born with Down's syndrome—a condition that leaves a child severely mentally retarded. Hospital officials deny the validity of the documents and refused to discuss what they called 'private and personal medical decisions' in public.

"The documents identify the child as 'Baby Boy Kelly.' The hospital also refuses to reveal the identity of the parents.

"The doctor who delivered the baby was quoted as saying, 'We will not allow a circus atmosphere to intrude upon the grief of these parents—the people's "right to know" stops where their privacy begins.'"

During the text of the news story, the station broadcast footage of Jason's family and Alvin at the press conference. At one point, Alvin was shown handing the copies of his evidence to reporters. The last segment of the story showed Daniella with a microphone being held before her. She said, "Jason is no criminal; he only wants to protect life. He took the baby because the baby would die if he hadn't."

"That was the best coverage yet," Alvin said to Daniella as he flipped off the set.

"They sure skipped a lot," Daniella added. "Like the fact

that the baby's atresia has been taken care of, and he is eating normally."

Alvin seemed to be thinking. Then he said, "Don't expect them to tell it all. They are just interested in the conflict—but be ready for the talk shows that want to hear from us in the next few days. Have them schedule any interviews through me. Give me a copy of your schedule so I don't cross things up."

"Just make sure you give me plenty of advance notice if you plan to do anything on a weekday morning—that's when I home-school Richie and Monica. Other than that, with Jason gone, I don't have a whole lot of plans."

●

June 28

Alvin,

Check with the Kellys on what they would do if the baby is returned to them. Would the same "treatment" continue? Would they adopt him out? Would they keep him?

I may be prepared to bring him back if he'll be safe. Sbnfhachowmaco.

In Christ,
Jason

The letter arrived through a hand delivery at Alvin's office. He knew it was genuine. Alvin had his sources and began to put out feelers for an answer to Jason's question.

●

"I wish you had spoken to us before talking to that reporter, Mr. and Mrs. Kelly," the man from the district attorney's office said. "We understand that Crabb is checking on what you would do if the infant were returned. He may even surrender if he feels the child is safe."

"I had no idea," Pat Kelly said. "I thought if he had found us that everyone probably knew where we were, and there was no use hiding any more."

"We've spoken with the station manager and the reporter on the matter, and they will keep quiet—for the time being." The assistant D. A. emphasized the last words. "The interview was aired only once—and that on a tiny station at about 4 a.m. We can only hope that word doesn't get to Crabb of what you said about continuing the same treatment."

Robert looked wide-eyed at the man. "You mean you don't know where he is at all? There's no progress on the case?"

The assistant D. A. responded, "We got a court order to look at his bank activity on the days surrounding his disappearance. From his bank machine withdrawals, it looks as though he probably headed north—toward Portland or even Washington. We think we may have cause to ask the FBI in on this case since interstate crime is their bailiwick. We haven't been able to get a wiretap permit on his attorney—we know they are in contact, but we don't know how.

"Anyway, I feel you should play along with anything that might get him to surrender. Contact his attorney if you must. You'll probably have to go public on this, too. The press has been real sympathetic to you and your rights to choose medical treatment for your child and rights to privacy. There's no reason why they should not continue to be."

•

The panel discussion on "The Town Meeting" television show included Alvin Toley, but it was a set-up. Another panelist was Jameson Durante, Ph.D. and some other alphabet soup behind his name. Durante was a bioethicist. The Reverend Slack was also on hand to pronounce his religious blessings on the ethical conclusions. And there was Martin Bongeur, the legal expert from the American Civil Rights Association—often called the A.C.R.A. Taped segments of an interview with Robert and Pat Kelly were preselected to salt the ethical performance. The moderator was anything but moderate in his views.

As the introduction for the show ended and the serious-sounding music dimmed, the moderator looked up from his papers and said, "Good evening. Welcome to 'The Town Meeting.' Tonight we will be discussing the strange case of the child abduction in Salem, Oregon, with a host of experts in legal and ethical issues raised by the case—and with the attorney for the accused racketeer and kidnapper, Jason Crabb. We will also, for the first time, be introduced to the anguished parents of the baby, Robert and Pat Kelly, via videotaped interview.

"We'll begin that after these words."

The monitor went to a commercial, and Alvin restraightened his tie. He looked around at the other panelists as they smiled and joked with one another. *It's strange how they can put on their "compassionate" faces only seconds before we go to air and drop them instantly when the red light goes off the camera,* he thought.

Studio workers fussed with the guests' microphones, and a woman with a soft brush powdered Reverend Slack's nose. The producer called out, "Thirty seconds!" and the extra bodies scurried away. The producer then began his ten-fingered countdown.

The host received his cue and began. "Tonight we discuss the Baby Boy Kelly kidnapping with the kidnapper's attorney, Alvin Toley; Dr. Jameson Durante, a medical ethicist; Martin Bongeur, a legal expert from the A.C.R.A.; Reverend Slack, an expert in religious ethics; and a taped interview with the baby's parents, Robert and Pat Kelly. This will be the first public appearance of the Kellys. Let's go to a segment of that interview first."

The studio monitor switched over and showed a couple in their late twenties sitting on a divan. Behind them was an impressionist painting which might have been an original. Pat was a slender woman with a rather ordinary shade of brown hair but extraordinary green eyes that were bright and hard—but her eyes were reddened now. Robert had settled back and seemed to blend in with the background as Pat sat erect. His demeanor seemed passive. His hair, like that of his son, was a dark, unruly mass covering his head. He seemed to be nervous about the whole affair.

"What I don't understand," Pat said, her voice on the edge of a sob, "is this man accusing us of wanting to kill our son. This was no easy decision for us. We decided against treatment for the throat blockage after a lot of soul searching and . . . and . . . well, we just didn't believe our son would be able to have a good quality of life."

Robert then leaned forward and said, "What makes me angry is that we as parents are supposed to have the right to choose medical treatment for our own child. Now, this Jason Crabtree, or Crabb, or whatever, decides to play God with our son. If you ask me, the boy is probably dead at Crabb's hands by now. What's it been? Three weeks? And he is afraid of a murder charge. What is difficult for Pat and me is not knowing. It is like having a runaway child or one that is missing in action in a war. You just can't lay it to rest."

Alvin could feel the almost palpable rise in sympathy for the Kellys. The host swiveled around in his chair as the monitor switched back to a studio shot of the group.

"It seems to me," the host said, "that the Kellys have made an agonizing decision—one of many possible, but one they thought best for the child. Your client, Mr. Toley, added to their grief by kidnapping the child. Could you respond to that?"

Alvin knew it would be a wasted effort to try to emphasize that Jason had *allegedly* done the deed or to argue the points of what was and was not kidnapping. He could see the danger if he, in any way, portrayed the Kellys' feelings as trivial.

"Making medical decisions for small children is always laden with the rawest of emotions—agony. Often, though, we make decisions without realizing what they actually *mean* in real life. As much grief and agony as the Kellys experienced in making this decision, it can't compare at all with the starvation and thirst the child would have suffered as a result. They may not have known this, but the net result of denying the boy surgery was starvation and thirst."

Up to this point, no one else spoke. Suddenly, the bioethicist Durante jumped in. "Mr. Toley makes a lot of grand statements and uses inflammatory rhetoric such as 'starvation,' but the reality is that the Kellys are a courageous couple who simply know when it is right to give up the extraordinary medical measures and allow someone—in this case their newborn son—to die. Mr. Crabb may have felt that the Kellys' decision was not the one he would make. Perhaps he would even want the child—and everyone else—

to have to live on machines if need be, but this does not permit him to play God with someone else's life."

"I hardly think it is 'playing God' to try to save someone's life," Toley shot back. "On the contrary, I would think that it is 'playing God' to decide when someone's life should end."

The moderator had a gleeful look in his eyes as the conversation began heating up—it was *great* television. "Reverend Slack?" he asked. "What about this 'playing God'?"

Somewhat pear-shaped, Slack had a balding pate sparsely covered with a few strands of hair left from a nearly dissipated widow's peak. He wore a tweed coat with elbow patches in an attempt to look the intellectual. His physique conspired against the image—victoriously.

Slack cleared his throat. "It seems that Mr. Toley, like many with a misunderstanding of God, makes physical life almost an idol. Death is *part* of life, and, while it may be tragic for those left behind—and especially in the case of the death of a child—the Christian tradition tells us that these go to eternal bliss with God. Other traditions say that death is an illusion and that the soul of the departed goes on to enter a new—and perhaps better—body. In either case, both traditions hardly call for the inordinate idolatry of physical life that Mr. Crabb seems to have embraced. His unwillingness to accept the universe as it is—death and all—and his seeming desire to recreate the world to suit his predilections would seem to be the ultimate in 'playing God.'"

"Even more to the point," Bongeur, the legal expert added, "the supreme courts of many states have repeatedly ruled in favor of parental decisions. Mr. Crabb—according to law—is perfectly free to believe his own way and to make medical decisions for his *own* children according to those beliefs. That's part of his religious freedom. But when he seeks to impose his religious choices on the lives of others, his freedom is nonexistent."

Toley grabbed the floor. "It's most interesting that you as an A.C.R.A. representative couch it in such terms, since it was the A.C.R.A. that recently fought to remove custody of a child from a family that believed in spiritual healing. In both of these cases, the parents freely chose to refuse treatment; in both cases, the perceived likely outcome was the death of the child. And in the other case, it was certainly a matter of what you have just described as a religious choice, yet now you stand on the opposite side. It was you, I believe, who finally succeeded in getting custody away from the parents, wasn't it?"

Bongeur's face visibly flushed, and there was an awkward silence. Durante reentered the fray to save the flustered Bongeur. "Mr. Toley has indicated that the Kellys' feelings in this are unimportant—"

Toley cut him off. "I didn't say 'unimportant.' I said that no matter how deep their agony, it does not justify starvation of an innocent child—and that's precisely the effect of their decision whether they understood that or not."

The host called for a commercial break and then resumed with another poignant segment of the Kellys' interview. The rest of the program seemed to rehash much of what was already said with Bongeur, Durante, and Slack attempting to focus on "complex details" and Toley dragging the conversation back to nagging essentials such as starving babies.

When Alvin left the studio, he was tired, but he knew he had accomplished something—he didn't know what, but something.

•

A viewer sat in the darkened room and watched the closing credits for "The Town Meeting" roll across the small screen. The video beside it read "REC" as it silently taped the remainder of the program.

I'd better look that lawyer up, he thought. *He needs a copy of that other tape.*

5

Harvey Moskowitz was old for an FBI special agent. People in the Bureau looked at him and wondered why he still was on the low end of things. The truth was that Harvey loved field work. He had no patience for the political infighting that went with the higher-classification territory. Not that he was a slacker. He could deal dirt with the best of them—shade the truth here and maybe an outright lie if necessary—but Moskowitz never felt compelled by a predatory instinct to initiate this kind of battle. He could be a powerful political street fighter, but he reserved the talent for defense.

Harvey was standing erect to his full five-foot, ten-inch height as he looked out the window on the small patch of grounds before the second story of the Salem office. There was something faintly military in his stance, although he had only briefly served in the military. His hawklike features and leathery skin reminded people of some rangy bad guy in a spaghetti western. His dark brown hair, with touches of silver along the sides, slicked straight back from his slightly receding hairline only accentuated the image.

The phone leaked a loud metallic chirp. Harvey snapped up the receiver. "FBI."

The soft voice on the other end belonged to Tom Myers, the assistant special agent in charge, called the ASAC in the Bureau. He was the FBI's number two man in Oregon. "Harv? We just got official request to come in on this Kelly baby case down there. The boss says to go ahead. You up to speed on what's happening on that?"

"Absolutely," Harvey responded. "The local boys have kept me informed on the basics. I guess they have some indication he may have left the state—but I don't think so."

"The boss says not to worry about that," Myers reassured him. "St. Luke's, the hospital where the baby was taken, is heavy on the federal dole. The boss says that probably gives us grounds—at least for a start. I hear the real story is that the kid's father is some bigwig and a son-of-another-bigwig in the timber industry and lives cozy by one of the U.S. senators."

"No difference to me," Harvey said with a cynical bite. "I just do the jobs the boss gives me. Every once in a while I get one that sounds like it will be an interesting case for my memoirs—and this sounds like one of them. I'll give my friends in the local departments a call and get the latest dope on this case, OK?"

"Sounds good, Harv," Myers said. "Keep us apprised. If you need anything . . . "

"Yeah, I'll just whistle," Harvey added. *Apprised,* Harvey thought, *why does Myers always use words like that*? He shook his head and hung up. Then he dialed the local police.

"Salem Police."

"Give me Detective Bob Hale, please."

●

July 8

Jason,

The Kellys are making noises like they will let the baby be adopted out if you bring him in. They sound sincere, but there is no way to be sure.

The feds have been called in on the investigation. Some say you've crossed state lines. Local FBI guy named Moskowitz says he'll handle the details of handing the baby over if you wish. Pray about it.

The RICO case is still going great guns. I guess they won't be able to depose you for a while, but the opposition is trying to have you held in contempt and defaulted. Since this is federal, it could get messy.

I've enclosed a letter from Daniella and the kids.

Hhtwtthachnsttp.

Yours,

The letter was signed in the large, distinctive hand of Alvin Toley. Jason barely glanced at the signature before flipping to the letter from his wife. He carefully read every line twice as if to draw her very life out of the penned words.

Getting up, he walked into the living room where the Oberstraats were.

"I don't mind facing the courts on the charges," he told them, "as long as Victor is assured of safety."

Wanda looked at him with understanding. "Well, you can't afford to be mistaken on this. Let's pray for guidance and ask that God will cover us if we make the wrong choice— the Bible says He's both our shield and our rear guard."

Just as they began to pray, a cry came from the back room where Victor lay napping. Jason was on his feet. "I'll be back in a sec. You start without me."

•

The female announcer's voice came over the radio saying, "It has been learned today that the FBI has become involved in the Baby Kelly kidnapping. Authorities say that the alleged kidnapper and racketeer, Jason Crabb, has fled across state lines and may have violated other federal laws as well. There is still no official word on the whereabouts of Crabb, but sources close to the investigation indicate that there may be a break in the case soon."

Harvey Moskowitz listened carefully to the broadcast and thought disgustedly, *That's the ticket. Tip the guy off that we're on to him. If Crabb hears that he may rabbit across state lines, and we could lose him for good—and just when he may turn himself in.*

Moskowitz knew there was no sense calling the station about such things. They would react with characteristic paranoia and mistrust of government agencies. *It would probably—in their alleged minds,* Harvey thought, *just confirm their statement and ring the censorship bells. They would make even a bigger deal of that.*

Harvey turned back to his work. He hoped that Jason would make it simple and turn up voluntarily—especially now that he knew the baby would be safe. Harvey had talked to the Kellys and their attorney a couple of times, and he felt that he could clearly tell Crabb that.

Still, he doggedly pursued his other leads. Harvey was convinced that Jason was still in the area. An informant who liked to sit around listening to a radio scanner, had picked up part of a phone conversation that indicated that Jason might be just east of town. Most people who own cordless phones were unaware that they were making a public radio broadcast that could be monitored by anyone with the money for a scanner. Wiretap laws did not apply as clearly to these "cordless" conversations.

•

"This fake ID looks pretty good, Jason," Tim remarked. "And the car we bought under your new name is registered to the same address down in Turner as the license."

"Yeah, but it looks like we won't need it now," Jason said.

Tim and Wanda looked surprised. "I think I'm going to take Victor in to that FBI guy, Moskowitz, Alvin told me about," Jason added.

"Are you sure?" Wanda asked as she looked up from the sleeping form of seven-week-old Victor who was curled up in her lap.

"I think so," answered Jason with a pained look. "I'm going in tomorrow in my old car. I'll call this Moskowitz from downtown so they don't know where I've come from. I'll leave the phony ID here with you so I don't get into more trouble because of it—and I'll sign the other car's ownership over to you. OK?"

Tim looked worried. "I suppose, but—"

"You heard the radio," Jason interrupted. "The FBI may be closing in on where I am. I don't want to involve you in the legal problems—and besides, the Kellys have said they will adopt Victor out."

"What I was about to say," Tim added, "was that both

Wanda and I really have felt a warning in the Spirit about that move."

"Tim, I respect your counsel—but I don't think you're right on this."

Wanda spoke cautiously, "Jason, I've noticed how depressed you've looked the last few days. Maybe you are just tired of this whole thing and want to get it over with and see Daniella and the kids again? Could that be it?"

"Maybe," Jason admitted. "But I feel I have to play this one through."

●

Alvin Toley picked the oddly wrapped package out of the mail pile. *Not a bomb, I hope.* He was thinking about the threatening phone calls and mail that had come since Jason had taken off with the baby—especially after "The Town Meeting." The small package was clumsily wrapped as though by a child, and the ragged scrawl of the address was difficult to make out.

Alvin took the package to his office. *If it blows up, at least it will only get me*, he thought only half jesting.

Inside the wrapping was a cassette tape and a letter from a dot-matrix computer. It said:

Dear Mr. Toley:

Please forgive the writing on the package and the wrapping job. I have cerebral palsy, which makes it difficult to do things well with my hands.

I saw you on "The Town Meeting" show the other day, and I agree with you. I have several radios and two TVs and try to keep up with all the slippery-slope deathmaking activities. Often I tape these things, and I'm up at odd hours so I hear lots of stuff.

This is a tape from a small radio station's early morning broadcast which you may find interesting. It sounds as if the Kellys plan to kill the kid even if he comes back all fixed up. Sounds sick to me, but listen for yourself and see if that's what it sounds like to you.

I don't know if this will help at all, but just in case it would, I sent it.

Yours truly,

And there was the same scrawly hand for a signature followed by a typed name, address, and phone number.

Alvin looked at the tape, which was labeled with a dot-matrix listing of the time, date, and station call letters. He removed the old Dave Brubeck tape, dropped the new cartridge into his office tape deck, and punched the "play" button.

The brief interview began after a station identification segment and started on an innocuous note. Suddenly, the question arose.

"What will happen to the baby when he is recovered from Crabb? Will there be a change in his treatment?" the reporter asked.

Pat Kelly's voice came through strongly, "My husband and I—and our doctor—made a difficult decision initially. Since then, we've talked further with the doctor and decided to continue with the original decision. It's all very painful for all of us, but we feel this is the best decision."

Alvin snapped off the tape and headed for the door calling to his receptionist, "Be back in a little while. Hold off my appointments with your charm."

Alvin knew he would be risking a lot to call the

Oberstraats from his house—or any pay phone around his office. Any of them could be bugged. Wiretap permits on attorney phones were difficult to obtain—because judges too were attorneys—but it was not impossible.

Alvin hopped into his trademark red Corvette and drove off. After satisfying himself that he was not being followed, he drove toward the state capitol building and pulled up to a single phone kiosk. "I wonder what ever happened to booths?" he asked himself aloud.

He dropped his coin in the slot and punched in the number. From the other end came the sweet voice of Wanda Oberstraat. "Wanda," Toley said abruptly, "this is Alvin Toley. Got an emergency. Can I talk to Jason?"

Wanda sounded distressed. "He just left, Alvin. He's going to see the FBI."

"That's what I was worried about. Can you catch him before he gets to town?"

"I think so. I'll get Tim to try."

Alvin pulled his small Bible from his coat pocket and rifled through the pages at the back. He said, "Tell him I said the Kellys still plan to kill the baby—I have proof. He's got to leave the area. Now! Here, take this down—do you have a pen?"

Wanda indicated she did.

"Write this: V-M-P-H-I-T-O-P-O-T-D-W-I. Got that? Yeah, W-I, that's right. Give that to him when you tell him. You've got to go right away."

With that Alvin hung up. He looked heavenward and prayed that the Oberstraats would catch Jason in time.

•

The old Dodge clattered down the twisting section of MacLeay Road heading toward the outer edges of Salem a few miles away. At that same instant, the Oberstraats pulled out of their gravel drive in a cloud of dust and sped toward the main road.

"Don't get us killed," Wanda said as they rounded the corner, the car tentatively holding onto the pavement of MacLeay.

"Wanda, if you only knew of the driving I've had to do covering some of those overseas stories."

"And I don't want to know," Wanda interrupted. "Just drive well this time. It's too important an assignment to lose on a wreck."

Tim fixed his eyes on the road, and Wanda watched for the dilapidated Dodge ahead. After several miles, she shouted, "There he is! Up there!"

"I see him," Tim answered. "Good thing he's not in a hurry or we'd never catch him. I think we'll get him."

Tim floored the accelerator and barely slowed for the stop sign at Cordon Road. They were only a block behind Jason when they reached the sudden right bend in MacLeay. When the Dodge began to pull away from the next stop at Pennsylvania Avenue, Tim began to lay on the horn. He could see the puzzled look on Jason's face as he rounded the corner going toward Lancaster Drive. Jason's face lighted with recognition, and he pulled his car to the curb a block down the road.

Tim pulled his vehicle in behind the Dodge and jumped out. Wanda watched from the car as Tim gestured and spoke to Jason—and finally handed him the torn corner of paper with the strange sequence of letters. Jason looked at the scrap and nervously scratched his bearded jaw. He said something to Tim and walked back to the Dodge and leaned into the driver's seat for a couple of moments. Soon he was back with Tim, and they discussed some more.

Eventually, Jason went back to the Dodge, and Tim returned to Wanda. "He's going to dump the Dodge here so it won't be found at our house," Tim said. "He's coming back to the house and will have to pack and take off. I think I can make some arrangements for him."

"What about the paper? What did it mean?"

"Probably some kind of recognition code with Alvin," he answered. "The less we know, the better, on things like that."

6

Jason and Victor, now James and Victor Cramer, drove down out of the lush hills in the Mt. Shasta region onto the floor of California's interior valley. Their plain-looking Ford van had panel sides, and only the rear doors had windows. Its interior was sparse, but it could sleep them both in a pinch. Jason had put in some time on the engine in the week and a half before they were forced to leave. It fairly purred along without strain as they came out of the hills. Once past Redding on I-5, the terrain was flat forever before them and flat for miles to either side until it met the massive, brown rolling hills that surrounded the state-long tableland. Barbed-wire fences stitched together the fields that threatened to engulf the broad concrete strip. Occasionally a small sign on a fence post proclaimed, "Wheat," "Oats," or some such crop.

The highway sign read, "Red Bluff 2 1/2." The gurgling coming from Victor for the last half hour became more agitated. "Just a couple of miles, little, and we'll stop for a while," Jason said soothingly as he began to reach up to deal with the tickle beginning on his chin. Remembering

Tim Oberstraat's warning, he brought the hand back to the wheel, its original mission canceled.

Tim and Wanda had refused any compensation for his stay or the car they bought him. He still had the original $900 he had started with. Alvin had sent him another $1,000 while he was in hiding at the Oberstraats. A little of that had gone for motel accommodations at a small group of cabins near Weed, California, where they had spent last night. Breakfast had done little to dent the large wad of bills. The proprietor of the ancient motel was also owner of the roadside cafe.

He asked Jason, "Where is the little woman?"

"Still up north."

The manager eyed him suspiciously and pressed, "It's not usual to see a man alone with a baby so young, Mr. Cramer."

"That's true," Jason answered. "But things are a mess up there, and there are some things that had to be cleared up before she can come to be with me and Victor."

The man looked satisfied, but the incident had made Jason realize that he needed a well-thought-out cover story. It reminded him of how he missed Daniella. She would be able to help him word a story so that it seemed he was spilling his guts but actually would be giving no substantial information.

Victor's discomfort grew appreciably as they pulled off the highway and found a gas station in Red Bluff. Jason took care of the baby's needs, and then looked again at the name and address Tim had given him. "I'll call him on the radio," Tim had said. "He knows people down in southern California and will set you up."

While traveling Jason had no way of communicating with Daniella and the kids or Alvin. He was anxious to find a place to settle for a few days so he could talk with Daniella again—and find out his and Victor's current status from Alvin.

The final hurried note he had scrawled to Daniella had hardly conveyed his disappointment about having to go on the run. It seemed more like a brief weather report. He had not had time to include one for Alvin, but he sent her note through the attorney.

●

Daniella looked up from the short letter from her fugitive husband. "Do you suppose you could now explain these curious words at the end of Jason's letters?" she asked. "What does v-m-p-h-i-t-o-p-o-t-d-w-i mean?"

Alvin looked thoughtful. He leaned forward in his chair and took the letter from her. "When Jason first left, he called me and we had a long talk. We came up with a code to help us determine if our letters to each other were genuine. It will also work with phone calls in a pinch. Anyway, at the time, I didn't tell you because the fewer of us who knew it, the better. But now things are more complicated, and it may be necessary for you to communicate with Jason directly at times—and perhaps these precautions will be necessary between us sometime."

"I can appreciate the need for it," Daniella said as she picked up James from the richly carpeted floor of the attorney's office and swung him onto her lap. She looked into his eyes and said, "Sit with mama, Jimbo." She kissed his forehead and continued, "How does it work?"

"Actually, it's pretty simple, Daniella," Toley said as he drew a New Testament out of his coat pocket. "This New Testament with Psalms and Proverbs is the key. It is a *New*

American Standard translation—and that is important. Jason has a similar one. The key is the date on which the letter is written. Look here on your letter. It is July 14—seventh month, fourteenth day. I turn to Proverbs 7:14 and look at the first letters in all the words in the verse. They are reversed as one word at the end of the letter—thus, v-m-p-h-i-t-o-p-o-t-d-w-i. If somehow Jason were under duress, or the information in the letter were false, he would not put the code on, or the code would be wrong."

Daniella looked at her watch. "Monica has a dental checkup in an hour," she said absently. "But, tell me, that chapter has only twenty-seven verses. What happens if he has to write on the thirtieth?"

"We decided to use the last chapter of Proverbs for that situation. We will just use the verse number corresponding to the day number as before."

"Pretty clever, Alvin," Daniella said.

"I can't take the credit there, Daniella. It was actually Jason's idea. I just helped develop some of the refinements. It will work all right as long as the FBI or someone doesn't get hold of too many samples of the notes.

"But there's something else I need to check with you. How are your funds holding out? I've got about $8,000 in the Crabb fund—we've got some generous givers out there. I sent $1,000 to Jason before he left."

Daniella looked a little embarrassed. She and Jason had always been self-sufficient—besides being givers themselves—and it was uncomfortable for her to have to be on the receiving end. Alvin noted the flush in her cheeks. "Christ gave us salvation, Daniella. We couldn't get it ourselves. Sometimes we must learn to be gracious receivers—just to remind us who our Provider is."

Daniella nodded. "Without the sale of one of the cars or

some other outside help, we will probably be needing money in about a week. I'll let you know."

"All right," Alvin said. "The people who put Jason and the baby up say he left with nearly $2,000, so he will be OK for a while."

"I suppose you don't know which direction he took?"

"Even if I did, it is better not to say. You notice I never told you where he stayed the last six weeks? The fewer who know, the better, Daniella. That's the watchword."

"I understand," she said. She gathered up her diaper bag and purse and left the lawyer's office.

•

It was late in the evening when Jason pulled the dark blue van off the I-5 at the Katella Street exit. Victor sat burbling in the car seat and seemed enthralled by the passing lights and sounds. He waved his arms excitedly from time to time and let out a grunt or a squeal.

"Yeah, it must be pretty exciting from your point of view, huh, little?" Jason asked. "Now we have to find this guy Tim sent me to."

Jason looked about at the maze of streets, lights, and cars and decided to ask directions. He wheeled his van into the gas station, parked it, and leaned out the window. "Got any idea where I can find this address?" he asked handing the paper to the casually dressed attendant.

"Yeah, sure," he answered and pointed down the road. "Head down this way about a mile and hang a left—it's the fifth light. This street is about five blocks in. Can't miss it."

Jason nodded his thanks, backed the van around, and drove off.

The directions were accurate, and in about ten minutes

Jason pulled up in front of a low brown and tan ranch-style home. It had decorative wood on parts of the exterior, but was primarily stucco. The neighborhood was definitely middle class with neatly trimmed—though drying—lawns stretched out before each house like a patch of murky green carpet. Jason remembered an old '60s folk song about these kinds of neighborhoods—"all made of ticky-tacky, and they all look just the same."

The singular variation in this house was the tall "ham" antenna that stood behind it.

Victor had fallen asleep again. Jason stopped to watch the slow rising and falling of his chest and listen to the soft sound of his breathing. Again he marveled at how anyone could reject such a lovely—and loving—baby. Carefully, he unlatched Victor's little seat belt, wrapped the receiving blanket around him, and lifted him from the van. Victor stirred only slightly.

Jason carried his bundle to the door and pushed the doorbell. A faint sound came from inside, and soon a man in his late fifties swung it wide. He looked at Jason and Victor with puzzlement. Then recognition lightened his face. "You must be James Cramer," he said. He pulled back the blanket slightly and looked at the baby. "And this must be Victor. Come on in—I'm Terry Wyers. Tim told me you were coming. You'll stay here tonight, but I have things lined up for you. You're probably tired, so I'll show you your room."

Terry Wyers was a very heavy man. Only about five and a half feet, he weighed in the neighborhood of three hundred pounds. He sported a full head of slightly graying dark hair, and his eyes seemed to be permanently squinting with laugh lines extruding from their corners. Tim had told Jason that he was a manager of a finance company. "He is more than he seems though," Tim had added. "He used to have what one might call a 'special relationship' with the Drug Enforcement Agency while he worked in a banking firm. He monitored strange transactions for the earmarks of drug trafficking. I bumped into him—accidentally—after a major cartel bust."

Terry led the way through the living room and into the hall. Abruptly, he stopped and turned around. "Maybe you're hungry—are you?"

"No, just tired," Jason replied.

"OK. OK. We'll just get you settled for the night. You need anything from the car?" Without waiting for an answer, he continued, "Bathroom's over there." He pointed. "The wife has the bedroom all set up for you two—she's already asleep. Feel free to use whatever you need—and sleep in tomorrow. You'll need extra rest after that drive. Actually, I wasn't expecting to see you so soon. Thought maybe tomorrow sometime."

Jason found the room nicely cleaned with a small crib beside the single bed. He made a trip to the van for a few things and was soon sleeping as soundly as Victor, though more noisily. About 1:30 a.m., Jason awoke to low gasping sounds from the crib—the sounds Victor made whenever he awoke without something in his mouth—especially when he wanted food in his mouth. Jason had mixed some formula earlier. But first he checked, then changed Victor's diaper. Victor continued to complain more and more loudly about his empty mouth. Jason tried to quiet him with consoling sounds and hoped he would not wake the house. The bottle quickly followed the diaper change, and Victor was satisfied.

•

Harvey Moskowitz held the receiver to his mouth and spoke quietly to his superior, "Well, Tom, I think if Crabb hasn't bit on bringing the baby back by now, he's probably not going to. I'm not getting any leads on his location out east, but the attorney's movements of late seem to betray a change in situation—nothing overt, just subtle stuff."

Harvey listened for a moment to the voice on the other end, then replied, "Sounds like Washington is hot-to-trot on this case, Tom. What's up?" Harvey thought, *There must be a lot of heat from above on this one for you to be that peevish.*

"I'd say Crabb has probably left the state. But how far do we go on this one—call out the National Guard?"

There was a brief spate from the other end of the line, and the conversation ended. Harvey cradled the receiver and leaned back in his office chair. It was an old oak chair that he had rescued from the federal junk pile along with the oak desk that stood before him. He liked wood furniture, and he even stripped the layers of institutional green and gray paints that had hidden the beautiful stuff for years.

Now where would I go if I was dragging a baby along? Harvey asked himself folding his hands behind his head.

•

Jason smelled bacon. He came up with a start, and when he focused on the clock, it read 8:47. Instantly, he looked to the crib only to see the empty receiving blanket. Throwing his legs over the side of the bed, he grabbed his pants and pulled them quickly on. Still buttoning them together, he emerged into the hallway and looked toward the living room. There, framed in the rectangle of the hallway, sat a woman in a swivel rocker holding Victor with a bottle to his rapidly moving lips.

She looked up at him and said, "I didn't want to wake you, so I went ahead and brought him out here while he was still sleeping. I've changed him, and he's having breakfast."

"Speaking of breakfast . . ." A second voice came from the kitchen followed by Terry's head. "It will be up in a moment. Go ahead and clean up, and we'll wait for you." Then as though suddenly remembering something, he nodded his head toward the swivel rocker. "That's Judy, my wife. You didn't get to meet her last night. Anyway, how do you take your eggs, James?"

Jason paused momentarily at the unfamiliar name. "Hard," he replied. "Cooked through."

"Gonna have to get used to your name, my man," Terry said winking at him. "Even first thing in the morning." He then disappeared into the kitchen.

7

The TV newsman directly eyed the camera and spoke seriously, " . . . the Irish government is reported to be seeking to have Dr. Jones returned for his participation in an abortion ring in that nation. Abortions are still illegal in Ireland. Several U.S. pro-choice groups, including the American Abortion Action Group, have rallied to Dr. Jones's support and have secured a legal team to fight extradition and call for political asylum. Betsy Winkler, president of American Abortion Action Group, comments on the situation."

The carefully coiffed hair and mahogany face of Winkler appeared on the screen. Her eyes were glistening with urgency and commitment as she said, "Ireland is a nation headed back to the nineteenth century when all others are living in the twenty-first. Dr. Jones is an enlightened physician who risked safety and security to take up the cause of Irish women. We cannot allow him to be forcibly taken back to that barbaric nation."

The newsman's face returned. "A spokesman," he said, "for the Irish embassy in Washington, DC, denies any attempt at extradition for Dr. Jones.

"Today about three hundred pro-choice demonstrators chanted and picketed outside the embassy. Pro-choice groups say they plan to picket the embassy and demonstrate against the Irish government until it issues a declaration of freedom for Jones.

"In other news tonight, the FBI has broadened the search for a kidnapped Oregon infant. The kidnapper, Jason Crabb, a political radical and racketeer, took the newborn infant, known as Baby Kelly, from a Salem, Oregon, hospital over six weeks ago and is believed to have left the state. FBI Special Agent Harvey Moskowitz, who is overseeing the case, was asked about the Bureau's involvement."

Moskowitz's leathery face, which had been frozen in the panel with the caption, "Kidnapping Case," suddenly filled the screen. His mouth moved without sound for a part of a second, and then he came on with, "Under the Lindbergh Law, it is a federal crime to cross state lines during a kidnapping. We have notified all branch offices nationwide to be on the alert for this man."

The newscaster's face reappeared. A picture of Jason appeared in the inset screen behind him. It was an old picture—not very flattering either—that made him look greasy and tough.

Dorothy Thompson looked over at Jason and said with a grin, "Why, Jim, that looks a little like you."

Dorothy, in her mid-thirties, herded four children around her house all day. Her husband, George, was a plumber who worked long hours and had yet to arrive home for dinner. Terry Wyers had brought Jason to their home and arranged for him to stay there. The Wyers lived a few miles to the north. Jason could practically hit Disneyland with a rock— at least, he could see the Matterhorn Mountain ride from here if he looked between the trees. The former owner of

Dorothy and George's home had converted a portion of the garage into a small apartment. Jason and Victor were given these quarters. It was more like a bedroom with a kitchenette. A door led to the laundry room of the house. Beside the laundry there was a three-quarter bath—a shower, sink, and toilet—for his use. Having only a shower presented some difficulties in bathing Victor, but Jason devised a more-or-less-workable system.

"Jim" didn't comment on Dorothy's remark. Instead he seemed to be puzzling over something.

"Is something wrong?" Dorothy asked.

"It's just that story about the abortionist from Ireland," he said. "Weird."

"I'll say," Dorothy answered. "I only wish that coming to the U.S. couldn't be called 'an escape.' The last thing we need in this country is another abortionist."

"You have something there," Jason replied.

•

"Fed Ex package for James Cra-merrr," George called in nasal imitation of an old cigarette ad. He walked through the open door leading to the garage apartment. Jason was there on the bed cleaning up a hideous-looking, olfactory-assaulting diaper that Victor had filled to overflowing. Messy butt and all, Victor seemed pleased with the accomplishment as he gurgled and cooed squirming in the gooey stuff. Dad tried manfully to remove the messy cloth from his hinder parts without leaving unwanted stains elsewhere.

Speaking between the pins in his mouth, Jason said, "Juff put it ober on the dreffer, Deorge."

"You're so maternal, Jim. Babies first, business last," he

said as he dropped the package on the mahogany bureau and headed out the door.

The "business" was indeed last because Victor was not satisfied with the change of clothes. He wanted to be held—and nothing else would do. He rejected his bottle and squirmed continuously while Jason tried to settle him down.

"Might be he has a rash starting up," the voice came suddenly from the open door. Jason looked up in surprise to see Dorothy standing in the doorway. "Let me take him off your hands and check him, OK?"

As soon as Dorothy left with Victor, Jason took up the overnight letter. It was thick and bore an unfamiliar name at a Salem address. Turning the package over, he peeled open the tab and poured out the contents. To his surprise, there were three bundles of money—old, crinkled bills—held together with rubber bands and sandwiched between two pieces of cardboard. Jason's first reaction, though, was to pull out the letter from Daniella. She told of all the calls from the press and her refusal to give most interviews. The police were watching the house regularly, but it had gotten so obvious that the kids had made friends with one of the detectives. After that, the obvious watch had been replaced with something more covert and sinister. She wrote letters at Alvin's office so no evidence of the communiques would be at the house.

Enclosed were two photos Alvin had taken of the family. "He recommends you destroy them after a couple of days," Daniella warned. "He says they may give you away—I think he's right." One picture had a love note from her on the back, and the other had a note from seven-year-old Richard.

After reading Daniella's letter several times and spending

a time longing over the photos, he turned his attention to Alvin's letter and the mysterious pile of money.

August 25

Dear Jason,

I'm sure you have read Daniella's letter by now. Mind what she says about the pictures. I was reluctant to send them in the first place.

I have included a return Fed Ex envelope that is pre-paid to the friend who sent this to you. He will make sure it gets to me. Use the Fed Ex as an emergency. Regular mail to him should be sufficient for most things.

I know you are puzzled by the money. Your last letter said you still had $1,000 left, and that would last a while. I was going to send another $1,000, but as I was praying about it, it seemed the Lord was telling me to send $5,000. I asked why, and only sensed that you would soon need it. I recommend you keep it with you wherever you go. I know it won't be easy to hide such a collection of—as they say in the trade—small, unmarked bills, but you'll figure a way.

The ride may get rough here, so call on the Lord and trust His leading.

Fbwihtbswmtb.

Yours,
Alvin

•

Life in southern California for Jason and Victor shortly became relatively placid. The money Alvin had sent was safely tucked in several places—one in the van, another in the diaper bag, and yet another on Jason's person. They were all but forgotten. After the one national report on TV about the Baby Kelly kidnapping, there was little additional news, just a couple of small blurbs in the papers accompanied by that same awful photo that had appeared on the television. Jason was able to work as an assistant to George Thompson. He fetched and carried and generally did a lot of physical work on the larger jobs. But those jobs only had him "helping" a few hours a week, and then it forced Dorothy to take care of Victor, who could be a handful at times. Jason was painfully aware that his usefulness was limited and that his efforts hardly compensated for his room and board, so he supplemented his work with cash from his reserves.

Dorothy, whose sister was raising a Down's child of her own, quickly trained Jason in the proper exercises for Victor's motor development. "It will take him forever to learn to do anything on his own, like to roll over or walk, if you don't help him use his motor skills," she explained. Jason made sure the exercises were done and—as Dorothy insisted—even when he had to wake Victor up to do it. "Some babies, especially Down's babies, sleep excessively," she had said. "It's not entirely a good thing."

But daily routine wore at Jason's caution, as well as that of the Thompsons. When he attended church with them, he was able at first to blend into the large crowd. Soon, however, members of the congregation began to recognize him as a regular attender, greet him, and try to invite him to lunch or a prayer group. Victor was a particular attraction, and it was all Jason could do to escape before questions about his wife arose. He had formulated answers to those questions, but he knew that once those were asked and

answered, they would be followed by more. His first plan
had been to say, "She's no longer with us," as if to imply
that she was dead. But he revised it to, "I'm afraid that is a
long and difficult story" and hoped that no one would be
"insensitive" enough to ask for details. "Insensitivity" was
regarded as a deadly disease in these parts.

Jason had been feeling the need for Christian fellowship.
He had missed it since the Oberstraats and was anxious to
find more of the comradery among believers. The
Thompsons were not always the hit of the church because
of their commitment to pro-life work. Many reacted with a
roll of the eyes whenever George or Dorothy stood to speak.
You could almost hear the "not another abortion speech"
emanating from the upturned faces. Jason was familiar
with the response because, despite the occasional nature of
his pro-life efforts, he had been similarly labeled at his own
church.

After a few weeks with the Thompsons, Jason agreed to
attend a home meeting at the associate pastor's house.
Dorothy had consented to watch little Victor, so "Jim"
hopped into the van and took off toward the meeting.

The associate pastor's house was modest, though much
more comfortable than the Thompsons'. Jason looked in
through the window and could see that the room was
already quite full. Most were people he had already met.

"Hi, Jim," the pastor said as he opened the door. "Come
on in. This is my wife, Ellen," he said indicating the brunette
with the soft, rounded mass of curly hair. She was comfort-
ably attired in a dark green blouse and slacks. "She'll introduce you around."

Ellen took "Jim" by the arm, led him through several
introductions, and then parked him with a jocular group of
older men who seemed to have their own agenda—sports.

One of them, Bill, had been by the Thompsons' on several occasions since "Jim" had moved into the garage. The Thompsons always introduced "Jim" as "family," and, when pressed, George would say that the relationship was difficult to explain, but that Jim was related to his "Father." George was a master at introducing new topics at this point, and Jason had picked up on that ability.

"So," one of the men said, "Bill tells us you are from Orygone. I hear that's a beautiful place. What brings you to California?"

"Well, it's a little hard for me to get work up there," Jason replied. "I heard that there was work down here—besides getting to see the Padres in person." *Parry and thrust,* thought Jason.

The lights went on in their eyes, and they began an incredible multiple conversation replete with mysterious sports terminology that left Jason standing in the dust and completely diverted the focus from him. Jason actually had only a passing interest in sports outside of trout fishing, and the nearby Santa Ana River had no trout. The only life in that river was the sand flea.

Soon the pastor called the group to order and opened in prayer. Next he asked for individual prayer requests and began with a prayer for Jason and his job situation. After prayer, one of the men led a Bible study from the book of Acts—the latter part of chapter 4 and the beginning of 5—and followed the reading and commentary by asking for discussion. There was a lively but amicable debate on some points, which eventually wound up the meeting. Ellen, the pastor's wife, opened the doors to the dining area and offered refreshments.

Jason asked to be directed to the bathroom, and when he returned, he was quickly absorbed into a knot of people.

". . . still don't see that verse as representing any kind of socialism," one of them said. "The verse says it was *voluntary*—and besides, they gave their money to the apostles, not to Caesar."

"He's got a point," another added. "Even Ananias and Saphira knew that their property was entirely their own—to do with as they pleased. It was the attempt at lying to God that got them their punishment."

"But surely," said another, a younger man with a radical gleam in his eye, "there was a reason they started to share. Could it be that it was the will of God all along? Maybe God wanted them to live communally."

Jason spoke, "The only thing the passage says is that those who were able voluntarily sold property *as there was need*. There is no indication of true communal living. I think the reason for the sudden drawing together of the Body of Christ here is related to the growing persecution they saw coming after Peter and John were arrested. Even the text points out that the Sanhedrin were restrained in their punishment of the apostles by the fear of the people. Remember, there were many thousands of 'The Way' in town—a force to be reckoned with. I think the believers sensed that things would not be getting easier and banded together more closely."

"I never thought of it that way before," the young man replied.

The pastor had worked his way next to Jason just before he began his comments and now signaled him aside. Once alone, he said, "Jim, I think you dropped your wallet in the bathroom." He handed the leather billfold to Jason. It seemed to Jason that an odd and inexplicable shadow crossed the pastor's face. He wondered what was behind it.

For the rest of the time there, Jason caught the pastor looking surreptitiously at him.

When he finally left, he drove his car a way down the road and pulled over. He felt tense inside. *I wonder if there was something about my wallet?* He pulled out the billfold and began to look through it. He said aloud, "Oh . . . sorry, Lord." There in the front of the small selection of bills were the pictures of Daniella and the kids—*in front of the bills*, not behind where he had put them. *I should have listened*, he thought. *I've gone and blown my cover. I wonder if he will turn me in?* Jason remembered the look in the pastor's eyes. *Yeah, he will.*

8

Associate Pastor Bob Duggan looked like a pastor—dignified—and would have preferred Robert to Bob, but in this land of surf, sunshine, and casual ways, that was too much to hope for. So he was Bob. It was likely though that he would soon take over the pastorate. The present pastor, a popular speaker on the circuit, was about to leave. He had overstayed the usual five-year limit and would probably take up lecturing for a year or so before landing another, larger church.

Duggan felt a genuine responsibility and care for the congregation. There was no hypocrisy in his faith—but he was a product of his times. In another day he would have had seven or more children. As it was, he and Ellen were stalled at two and let it go at that.

Now he was faced with a complex issue. Since last night, he was sure that "Jim" was actually the kidnapper from Oregon. Previously, he had had the feeling he had seen the man before, but couldn't remember where. The pictures in the wallet triggered his memory of the newspaper article with the picture of "Jim" and his family. Though the regular news never said so, he had read about the attempt by the hospital to starve the baby, and it did not surprise him. The information was from a highly credible publication that dealt with pro-family issues produced near L.A.

There was no doubt in Robert's mind that what the hospital and the parents planned was murder. But was kidnapping the answer? No doubt, the radical pro-lifers such as the Thompsons would call it a "rescue," not a kidnapping. He was deluged with memories of the pro-lifers in his last church begging for church support—even just moral support—as they went on rescue missions to the abortion clinics. He could remember their screams from the video tape as police used pain-compliance holds indiscriminately on young and old alike. He clearly remembered the snap of one man's arm being broken when police used nunchakus, a martial arts weapon, to force him away from the death chamber door. Robert was deeply moved by it all, but he still was convinced that lawbreaking was not the solution. The battle, he felt, was to be won by preaching the gospel and by praying.

He wondered if the steps for confronting a sinning brother that Jesus listed in Matthew 18 were applicable. Should he go to "Jim" alone first and hear his answer? *No,* he thought, *he hasn't sinned against me—he's broken the law.*

Duggan could not bring himself to share this with his wife; he remembered all too well how she had responded to the tape of the man's arm being broken. *Ellen would respond emotionally,* he thought. *Besides, I want as few people as possible involved. We don't want the church in turmoil over this.* It was an issue he would have to deal with on his own.

Duggan could see the potential mess if he were to simply report "Jim." Many in the church, including himself, would be questioned by the FBI, and the Thompsons could be looking at some real legal trouble. He did not want to drag the entire church in on this.

Then it struck him—he had seen "Jim" at the grocery store the other day stocking up on formula. He had seen "Jim" there with the baby several times. He could report that. Maybe they would stake out the store and wait for him. Of course, that could still end with plenty of trouble for the Thompsons if they were able to trace him there. *But the Thompsons chose to get involved*, he thought. Duggan decided to leave it up to God whether their role was uncovered or prosecuted.

But he didn't want it known that he had leaked the information to the authorities. In a move of extra caution, he drove to a local phone booth.

"FBI," the voice on the other end said.

"I think I have some information about one of your cases," Duggan said. "But I want to be anonymous."

•

When Jason came back from the study, he immediately took George aside and told him of his suspicion about Duggan. A dark look crossed George's face. He leaned forward and put his hands over his eyes as if thinking it over. From behind his hands he said, "Jesus said that when we are persecuted in one city, flee to the next. I don't want to say Pastor Duggan is persecuting you, but he opposes pro-life rescues and no doubt will oppose your situation. It is possible he'll say something to the cops—that could get really sticky. I think you need to pack and go. I don't have anyone to send you to except a friend who will put a quick primer job on that van of yours. That will help you to be less visible."

"I really don't know which direction to head, George," Jason said.

"I don't either," George replied. "And it's better I don't because if things come down hard here, I don't want to know anything to tell the FBI. If Duggan talks, there's no telling how much he'll give them."

Jason went to pack Victor's things into the van while George looked for Dorothy. She was just coming out of the bedrooms where she had put the children to bed for the night. "We missed you for bedtime prayers, George," she said.

"Sorry, dear. Something came up, and I need to tell you about it."

Dorothy looked out the living room window and saw Jason loading the van with a box through the open doors. "I suppose it has something to do with that," she pointed.

"In fact, it does," said George. "I'm sending him to Hippie to get his van painted. I don't know where he'll go from there—it's better if we don't. Pastor Duggan got a look at his family pictures when Jim accidentally left his wallet in the bathroom. Jim says that Bob behaved oddly after that. We think he may turn Jim and Victor in. Anyway, we don't want to chance it—until now, God has always given Jim warning about when to run, and he does not want to be presumptuous of God's protection."

"Does he have any money?" she asked.

"As a matter of fact, he does," George said. "A few weeks ago, his contact in Oregon sent him a wad because he was sure Jim would need it. Talk about Jehovah-jireh."

•

National news moves in cycles. If a reported event stirs a response, more news on that issue will be reported, which may lead to more response, then more coverage.

So it was when the Baby Kelly story was shown on network news. It was the scant information given on the report that piqued the interest of a nationally known liberal columnist from Chicago. Several dozen phone calls and a sheaf of fax copies confirmed his suspicion that the story was much broader than the herd-journalists of the East Coast would lead the public to believe. Despite his generally liberal—even leftist—outlook, his studied pro-life position was apparent.

The columnist blasted the press for their sparse coverage of the facts and evasion of the crucial issues underlying the case. This piece gave leverage to the cries of anti-euthanasia groups, and suddenly their leaders were deluged with requests to appear on panel discussions. The Baby Kelly kidnapping (or rescue, depending on the speaker) began to appear as a third-level national story. The legal and ethical issues involved began to surface as viable topics of discussion. Naturally, the radio talk shows found it to be lively grist for their mills.

Baby Kelly was on his way to becoming a celebrity. This was *both* the good news and the bad news. National exposure gave the baby pathos and humanity—but it also spread far and wide the pictures of his protector, Jason Crabb. It made it much more difficult to hide.

•

Talk Show Host: It seems to me that it's parents who are responsible to rear and pay for their child. Hospitals are not allowed to do any kind of medical work on a minor without parental permission. And this was no easy decision for the parents. It was a private decision. Why should this Crabb guy step in and make those decisions?

Caller: Well, Peter, you're right about minors. They can't even get their ears pierced without their parents' permission—but they can get an abortion without permission.

Host: Now let's not get off the subject. We're not talking about abortion here.

Caller: Sure we are, Peter. It's just postnatal abortion, that's all.

click

Host: I hate to hang up on folks, but we need to stay on the subject. It seems that the anti-choice people see relevance to abortion in every topic we discuss. Let's get back to the Baby Kelly kidnapping. Next caller is Don. Hello, Don.

Caller: Yeah, Peter, you were saying that it was no easy decision for the parents.

Host: That's right.

Caller: My response to that is, so what? I mean, agonizing over it doesn't absolve anyone for doing wrong, does it?

Host: I guess not, but what I was driving at was that these people were traumatized by the decision itself. They didn't make this decision out of a selfish concern for convenience.

Caller: How do we know? I mean, I'm not accusing them of anything, but if they were motivated by selfishness, how would we really know? Would they admit that it was selfishness? Can we judge sincerity by how many public tears are shed?

Host: C'mon, now. Parents naturally love their children—especially newborns—and wouldn't have any reason to do anything that wasn't motivated by love for them.

Caller: Amazing, Peter! A liberal Pollyanna! Aren't you the same guy who thinks that most parents abuse their children and that the state should monitor parenting practices?

Anyway, Baby Kelly's parents love him with talk and tears; Crabb loves the baby with action and self-sacrifice.

•

Across the country the debate continued both publicly and privately. A rekindling of the pro-life movement seemed to be under way. Mounds of mail hit the Irish embassy, three-to-one in favor of Irish pro-life policies that could mean criminal prosecution for Dr. Sean Jones, the fugitive abortionist. The FBI was getting daily calls telling them to "leave Crabb and Baby Kelly alone."

Back in Oregon, Moskowitz watched the media coverage and received that tally of calls and mail with quiet interest. The description from the anonymous source in southern California said that Jason sported a mustache and goatee and short hair. Harvey had the office put together a photo with airbrushed changes and faxed them around the country with the vehicle description given by the source. *He has probably changed some of those features*, Harvey thought.

His thought was correct. Jason had dropped the beard, kept the mustache, and picked up a pair of low-power reading glasses which he wore in public. He scarred up the heavy black frames to make them look old and put tape on one of the hinges. He had heard once that having an unusual feature such as a bandage on the face or tape on the glasses drew attention away from one's actual appearance. People often remembered only the unusual feature and disregarded the rest.

After the paint job on the van, Jason took off directly towards Arizona on highway 10. Normally, Victor loved the rocking motion of the van and either slept or played quietly with the air in front of his face. However, this time after several hours, he became so cranky that Jason decided to pull in and take a motel room in the dusty border town of Blythe. The small, dingy motel was just a stone's throw from the murky Colorado River—which also constituted the Arizona border. Behind them was the long desert road between Indio and the border; ahead lay the longer desert trek to Phoenix.

Southern California had been strange enough for the Oregon-born mechanic, but he had been somewhat prepared for the lack of vegetation by the descriptions of California transplants. However, this desert, completely devoid of life, was hard on his eyes. He had always thought the eastern Oregon "deserts" to be harsh, but they were nothing like this.

The late August sun baked the land, and the small air conditioner sticking through the cinder-block wall of the motel room labored to keep the room just below sweltering. The long, hot drive made it impossible to continue with Victor's exercises, but Jason faithfully continued them whenever he stopped. Victor was already hot and sticky before the exercise, and after an hour of yowling, he fell into an exhausted sleep.

•

Twenty-five men and women stood with Alvin Toley before Judge Hiram Long. The trial was over, and the defendants had all been found guilty of Trespass II before a jury of their peers. Oregon law—a law designed to protect the victims of crimes—allowed the state to try the defendants *en masse*.

Long put on his sternest look as he passed sentence. "I feel you are guilty of something far greater than trespassing on someone's property—you are guilty of disrupting the social order. Your disregard for the laws and the rights of others—even though cloaked with religion and patriotism—is a threat to the very things you profess to uphold. I am sentencing you to the maximum allowable by law—thirty days and $500.

"And as for you, Mr. Toley, you are the worst offender. As a sworn officer of the court, you know better than to make a circus of the courtroom. I am giving you fifteen days for contempt of court for your attempts to drag religion and what you call 'baby killing' into this proceeding."

The judge was finished, but Alvin was not. The contempt finding was already at the beginning of its appeal process, so he would serve no time until that had taken place. He only wished he could tell the other twenty-five the same.

As he left the courtroom, he spotted his "tail." He found it hard to believe that these people actually thought they were succeeding in being inconspicuous. Fortunately, they only followed him intermittently. *Budget cuts,* he thought.

It had been a week since he had heard from Jason and Victor, and he was a little concerned. Glancing at his watch, Alvin recalled that he was to meet with Daniella and the kids this afternoon.

It was the day after Labor Day, and the sky misted and sputtered as though trying to fulfill some duty to rain the day after summer vacation ended. There was just enough wet to make goo out of the dust on the windshield, but not enough to get it clean. *That's why God made windshield cleaners*, he thought as he punched the button and the streams of cleaner sent momentary lines across the glass. He put his car in gear and headed toward his office.

Once there, he cleared this morning's cases from his briefcase and put them in the "out" box. He could hear the kids from the reception area when Daniella arrived. "Send them in," he said into the intercom. Soon the office was filled with the children, and Daniella sat quietly on the leather-covered chair.

"One of the networks wants me to come as a guest on an afternoon talk show, you know, Don Tinnamen," Daniella said without preamble. "I think it may be a good idea. They tell me that Dr. J. R. Lasant will be there—he is the best pro-life debater there is, so at least I won't be ambushed."

"When do they want you?" Alvin asked.

"Next week. They have even offered to pay our way— kids and all—in New York City for an extra day. It will make great schooling for Richard." She nodded toward the boy reading in the corner.

Alvin could see that despite Daniella's remarkable faith, the strain was beginning to take a toll. She missed Jason and, because no one had heard from him, she worried too. "OK," he said. "But I want you to take a break from some of this soon. I want you to use the house down at the coast for a week or so. Will your car make it?"

Daniella smiled and let out a small laugh. "I know the old beast looks bad, Alvin, and I've always wanted something that looked nicer, but Jason kept that car running perfectly. He always said that the car that most often carried me and 'the littles' should be safe and running right. Yes, it will make it."

With that, Alvin gave Daniella an update on everything he knew—and didn't know—about Jason's flight. She handed Alvin an envelope for the next communique and departed.

9

The old man almost seemed to rise out of the desert sands, but Jason knew it was an illusion created by the heat. He pulled over.

"Need some help?" he asked.

"Got all the help I need right here," he answered through the mass of whiskers—and *whiskers* was the word for it. *Beard* was too civilized a term for the tangled, gray bush that comprised most of his face. The man looked like he had just stepped out of an old western movie.

"Where are you going?" Jason attempted again.

"Depends on how far down the road of life you're talking about. For now, I just need to go a few miles from here."

"Well, hop in the back. The baby's asleep in the passenger seat."

The old man walked around the front of the van stirring clouds of dust with each step. He opened the side door and—more spry than Jason expected—hopped in.

"What're you doing way out here?" Jason asked.

"I live out here. What're you?" the man answered. "I do whatever I have to do. Cabin's up here a couple more miles and a quarter mile to the right. Look for the burial marker near the road and turn there. Lived alone for a long time—previous owner of the cabin is buried on the property. That's the burial marker."

He seemed to be testy and demanding. *No wonder he lives alone,* Jason thought.

They rode in silence until the van turned down the dusty track.

"You are a man with problems—I can tell," the old man said suddenly.

Jason looked over into his companion's eyes and was startled by a strange brilliance within their depths. The scratchy voice continued, "Why don't you stop over for a few days at my place. I got all the modern conveniences—an indoor water pump and generator."

Jason's initial caution seemed overcome by a remarkable sense that he could trust this man. "But—but I don't even know your name," Jason stammered.

"Butler," he answered as if anticipating the remark. "I'm just called Butler."

Jason looked over at Victor and was surprised to see him awake and apparently spellbound by the old man's face. He looked at Butler with his mouth agape. Butler looked down at the sweet little face and said, "Don't you worry, little Victor, we'll watch out for you. Just me and Jason."

It was all so natural that Jason didn't even recall that he had never given the old man Victor's name—or his own.

•

A patrol car sat below a small bluff overlooking the highway into Phoenix. The officer looked through tripod-mounted binoculars at every van headed east on highway 10. It was terrible duty, but the FBI had requested it. The chief had agreed to three days of daytime watch and close patrolling, looking for inbound Ford vans—possibly dark blue—possibly with Oregon plates. The special agent who requested the watch had a hunch that the Baby Kelly kidnapper was headed toward Phoenix and highway 10 was almost the only way to get there—or at least the shortest.

A hunch, the officer thought scornfully as he sat in the blistering heat. *Sounds like something out of an old cop show on TV.*

It was yet thirty miles to Phoenix, and this stretch was flat and straight enough to read plates. The disaffected officer spotted another van to the west. Dutifully he turned his field glasses toward the approaching vehicle, but by the time he had adjusted the focus, the van had disappeared. Looking again, the patrolman spotted the telltale dust cloud of a vehicle having turned off onto a dirt track. "Humph," the officer said aloud, "it's a gray van anyway." Realizing how dry his mouth was, he turned and reached for his thermos of ice water.

•

The cabin was surprisingly well kept. Jason's fears that there might be dirt floors—or just dirty floors—was unfounded. The old guy had a generator for power. A water tank partway up the hillside fed the house with water, and a European-style water heater was hooked up to both the shower and the kitchen sink. All of this was hidden from view, and the interior of the place still had the rustic appearance of pre-electric days.

"Make yourself and Victor at home," old man Butler said as he disappeared into the next room.

Soon Jason could hear the chug-chug of the generator

around back of the dwelling. Butler again entered the room. "There'll be hot water in a bit," he said. "I'm sure you'll want to clean up. You two can have the bedroom there," he indicated the door from which he had emerged. "I can take the sofa for a while."

"I wouldn't want to—" Jason began as he placed the gurgling Victor down on a blanket on the floor.

"Never you mind about me," Butler insisted. "I've been taking care of myself for a long time, just me an' the Lord. You take a blessing without complaint, you see?"

"OK," Jason answered. He looked at Victor lying on his back contentedly playing with the air before his face.

"I've got other work to do, so we probably won't see each other much while you're here, Jason. You just cook and clean like you would at home a few days, and I'll be happy. Take off when you've gotten rested up."

With that pronouncement, Butler walked out the door. At that moment, Jason realized that he and Victor had been called by their names—their real names. The most bizarre aspect of it struck him. Of the people who connected him to the rescue—the police, Alvin— nobody except him, the Oberstraats, and his friends in California had been told Victor's adopted name. He saw no television, radio, or even old newspapers in the cabin where the old man would have even become familiar with the story. Jason's curiosity got the better of him, and he immediately went outside to confront Butler with his question.

When Jason emerged into the brilliant afternoon sun, he could not see Butler anywhere. There was simply no way for him to get out of sight in that short time, unless . . . Jason ran to the other side of the cabin, but found no sign of the old man there either.

•

"George Thompson to see you, Pastor Duggan," the intercom chirped. Duggan developed an instant pit in his stomach. In some ways he had been expecting this. "Send him in," he answered.

George walked in and nodded toward the pastor. Duggan half rose and indicated the chair before the desk. But George stood.

"Did you ever read *The Hiding Place* by Corrie Ten Boom, Pastor?" he asked without preamble.

"Yes," the pastor nodded slowly, unsure of the direction of the conversation.

"There was a part in the story," George began, "where Corrie and her father are discussing hiding Jews with a local pastor. The discussion is all very academic, so to resolve that, Corrie brings a Jewish baby out to the pastor and asks if he would be willing to help *this* baby. The flustered clergyman sputters and finally declines to help because it would be breaking the law. The child was later taken by the Nazis and was never seen again. Do you remember the part, Pastor?"

Duggan could feel the heat rising as his face flushed. "Yes," he muttered.

"I probably needn't speak more plainly, Pastor, except to verify—you *did* turn in Jim and Victor, didn't you?"

The pastor held his head erect and looked directly at George. Finally his eyes sought the blotter on his desk. His lips tightened, and he nodded and croaked, "Yes."

"Did you really think God would leave it in the dark?" George asked. He waited momentarily, then left.

Duggan could now see with the clarity of a prophet. The turmoil in the church he sought to avoid, it was coming—

in spades! His hope for the chief pastorate—vanished! The word would go out—with or without gossip—and his credibility as a caring and confidential church leader would be demolished. The blot would follow him from church to church for years.

•

When she saw Alvin Toley after church, Daniella broke free of the group she was with and touched him on the arm. She pressed an envelope into his hand. "This is to go with the first mail to Jason—it's very important," she said.

He looked at her questioningly. She seemed shaken.

She added, "I wasn't sure for a while; then I didn't want to worry him, but Jason needs to know that he has another child."

Alvin deliberately stifled any visible reaction. "You're pregnant?" he asked quietly.

"Yes, about three months," she answered. "As near as I can figure, I conceived the night Jason decided to save the baby—almost seems like God's blessing on his decision. But it still makes it harder on him. I want you to tell him if he calls, otherwise send this."

"Are you still planning to do that network show?" he asked.

"Sure. Is there some reason not to?"

Alvin answered, "If they found out about your pregnancy, it wouldn't surprise me if they tried to drag that into the argument—make Jason look like he has abandoned his own responsibilities."

Just then a couple of women came up with bright smiles. "Oh, Daniella, is it true? I hear you are pregnant again?"

Alvin looked at her as if to remark, "See what I mean?"

Daniella acknowledged the truth of their information. *Word is getting out*, she thought. *I wonder if I'll get as much flak from the family-size monitors in the church this time? At least some of the older women support having large families.*

But Daniella had much more to worry about than the pressures of the pregnancy. Alvin had told her that the support fund for her and the kids was depleted—at least for the moment. It was the worst possible moment. She had already sold the three cars Jason had finished rebuilding before his unexpected departure. Now it looked as though she would have to begin selling the tools. She hated the thought because it had taken many years to accumulate them, and it was unlikely she would be able to get anywhere near their true value.

When this whole thing began, Daniella had been so sure that Jason was doing God's will, but now she—usually the stronger spiritually—was beginning to waver. She prayed—but seemed to hear nothing in return.

●

Jason had the van all packed with Victor's things. The old man had been right—in fact, Jason had not seen him once since he had walked out the door the first day. And either Jason's sleep was exceptionally sound, or Butler was virtually noiseless, because there was evidence that Butler slept on the couch, but Jason had never heard him come in.

Jason wrote Butler a thank-you note and was placing it on the table in the main room when he heard a noise outside. Quickly, he stepped to the door and saw Butler leaning in the van window saying good-bye to Victor. Suddenly, the old man turned and said, "You should have smooth going to Phoenix. But you need to be careful. You might find some help if you go to Encanto Park in town there."

Because of the pointed way Butler spoke, Jason was taken off guard. He had forgotten the questions he had planned to ask the old man when he saw him again. Once more the sense that he should trust this man overwhelmed his rational queries.

After a brief parting exchange, Jason hopped into the van and drove off slowly trying not to create too much dust. He directed the vehicle back on to highway 10 and accelerated toward Phoenix. Victor seemed pleased to be on the road again. "With all this road work so early in life, you'll probably grow up to be a traveling salesman, huh, Victor?"

It wasn't long before Jason noticed the breakfast he had not had this morning. He had fed Victor but, in his haste to get going, he did not want to cook for himself and have dishes to do afterwards.

The sun had barely come above the horizon, and the night chill of the desert had already evaporated like so much dew. The signs indicated that he was approaching Phoenix, but a roadside diner attracted his eye. Several pickup trucks were clustered around the cafe. It looked like the morning hang-out for local ranchers. He pulled in to the nearest side of the small building, unhooked Victor's seat, and carried him up to the glass door. Inside was a state trooper at the counter. Jason froze momentarily and looked around until he spotted the squad car on the opposite side of the block-walled diner. He knew that leaving now would look more suspicious than going on in, so he stepped into the air-conditioned coolness and found a booth at the far end.

The officer was at the stool nearest the old manual cash register and seemed to be getting ready to leave. The waitress was nearby, and the officer was saying, ". . . finally off that detail. Three shifts just standing in the heat all day. 'Pears that the FBI guy from Orygone was all wet on this one. Well, best I get back on the road, Mary. See you later."

With that he dropped a couple of bills next to his plate, stood and adjusted his gun belt, and strode out the door. "Bye, Merv," the waitress said as he walked out.

Jason heard the last remarks, but it did not occur to him that the special surveillance had been for him. Still, he was wary of law enforcement officers.

Mary, the waitress, soon appeared by his table with a menu and said, "Would you like coffee . . . say, there's a cute little bug." She leaned over to Victor in his car seat. "I didn't see you come in, handsome. You and your daddy here want some coffee?"

Victor's eyes were wide as he regarded the woman. There was no way of telling how he felt about Mary's overwhelming perfume. Victor gurgled and laughed. "See, there," Mary reported, "he likes me. Where's mama, little darling?"

Jason forced a smile. "Oh, she's working," he said. "This is just some man-to-man time for the boy and me."

"That's nice," Mary said genuinely. "Well, I'll leave you men alone and get your order in a bit, OK?"

She turned, not expecting an answer, and headed back to the kitchen area.

Without further incident, except a diaper change, Jason ordered and ate breakfast and was soon passing through the outskirts of Phoenix. Out of his pocket he pulled a letter he had written to Daniella—and another in it to Alvin. He was tempted to mail it to Alvin's go-between now, but he thought better of it. *I'd better get a return address I can use first,* he told himself.

He bought a city map at a gas station and got directions

to Encanto Park. There he parked in the lot, put Victor in the baby-knapsack, and set out to scout the territory. It was only around 10 a.m., and there were few people in the park. Jason noted a cluster of young people by the bandstand talking secretively and jabbing each other. *Those kids should be in school,* Jason thought. But when he got a better look, he realized they were a rough bunch, probably armed. He added, *No, they shouldn't.* An older man furtively approached the group. "It looks like the dope peddler has arrived," Jason murmured to Victor.

He wanted no trouble, so he steered clear of the area and began following the canal in the park toward the man-made lake. Soon he found a large tree, set Victor's carrier upright against it, and planted himself below it. "I wonder what we're here for, Victor."

Jason pulled out his little New Testament and began to read about Mary Magdalene from whom Jesus cast out seven devils. She was the first to seek Him out after the crucifixion—and first to believe in the resurrection. Jason always found it hard to believe that she had been a prostitute. He marveled at the passage and thought how the gospel had power to transform even the most difficult cases.

It was then that he noticed the boots—dull black boots that led into a pair of grease-slicked jeans. Above it all was the well-muscled torso of "the dope peddler."

"Got a light, mister?" asked the man.

10

Daniella and the kids walked into the Manhattan talk show studio. The network had flown the entire family in as well as Laurel Chambers, a young unmarried friend of Daniella's who agreed to help with the kids while they were in the big city.

A receptionist with auburn hair sat behind the gleaming black desktop. "May I help you?" she queried smiling pleasantly.

"I am Daniella Crabb—" she began.

"Of course. Allow me to get an escort for all of you." The woman leaned toward a touch pad, punched in a number, and spoke into the wire headset.

Her attention returned to Daniella. "Those are lovely children. They are all yours?"

Daniella beamed, "Yes, they are. This is Richard—he's almost eight; Monica is five; Nicole over there holding my friend's hand is three, and Jimbo here is about eighteen months. Then there's the one you don't see—little whosit." She patted her tummy.

"Five children. It must be a lot of work," the woman answered with a growing gleam of submerged envy in her eye.

"True enough," Daniella said. "But I would rather have kids than useless time."

Just then, the escort appeared. He wore gray slacks, a tie, and a dark blue blazer with the corporate logo stitched on the left-hand pocket. "Would you like to come with me, Ms. Crabb?" he asked.

"It's Mrs. Crabb," Daniella corrected. Then she smiled at him and added, "I suppose they have that Mzz stuff so drummed into you that it would be difficult to say anything else—say Mzz if you must."

They were quite early for the show. The make-up crew snagged Daniella from the group, put her in a swivel chair, and began to dust her with powder. They fussed and commented as though she were not there, but finally asked, "How do you feel?"

Daniella nodded as she looked at the strange new colors on her face in the mirror. Noting her dismay, the brush-wielding lady said, "Don't worry. The heavy lights wash out most of the color. You'll look just like you."

Another person entered the room asking, "She ready?" and proceeded to help her from the chair without waiting for an answer. "I'm Bob," he said, "and I'll get you wired up on the set. The studio audience and a couple of the other guests are already out there."

They walked through a corridor that suddenly broadened out into the studio. There, almost isolated from the madness of lights, wires, and cameras, was the main set. It floated like an island in the flat-black-painted surroundings. Before it bright linoleum flooring separated the main set from the audience. Daniella recognized the regal good looks of Dr. Lasant, her only protagonist on the panel. They would face Dominic Stanford, president of Americans for Medical Choice—a group best known for its advocacy of what they called "rational suicide and doctor-assisted suicide"; Dr. Elgin Chapman of the Holloway Institute for Medical Ethics (the network's tip of the hat to a centerist point of view); and Reverend Thom Hillyard, author of *God in the Tough Decisions,* a patently pro-abortion and euthanasia tome popular with the quasi-religious public.

People flitted urgently through the room carrying equipment or sheaves of papers. The floor director was speaking into his headset and pointing toward a lighting group.

Lasant sat to the right of center stage, and Stanford sat to the extreme left. Bob led Daniella to the center seat and pulled up the small mike. "Go ahead and have a seat here, and we'll hook this up," he said. He accomplished the task quickly and left.

Dr. Lasant nodded towards her and introduced himself, as did Dominic Stanford. The others soon emerged from the corridor, were arranged on the set, and plugged into microphones. A woman came soon afterward and had each one do a sound check by talking naturally. Her headset informed her when the adjustments were made, and she disappeared.

Don Tinnamen, the show's host, entered and introduced himself to the panel. He spoke briefly with them before turning and walking through the audience. They loved his banter with them, and he was able to identify who represented the subtle sides of the controversy.

Someone said, "Three minutes!"

•

Jason sat on the old musty couch swapping diapers on Victor's hyperactive bottom. "You're really going through them today, kid," he told the squirming baby.

The interior of the dope peddler's small cinder-block house was decorated in "early garage sale"—very early. It turned out he was not much of a dope peddler. He was called "Quinn" by everybody—his surname was Roberts, and he had lived on his own mostly since he was fifteen years old. "My dad officially tossed me out after I turned fifteen," he explained. "Good thing he had taught me to weld before he did, or I would'a had to work the streets, ya know what I mean." After remarks like this, he would laugh, "Hu, Hu."

A product of a criminal family, Quinn had spent some time in juvenile homes and even did a stint in the penitentiary. He had learned to fend for himself quite handily. Quinn's dark brown hair was mostly straight and tended to fall across his eyes when he didn't keep his head slightly tilted back.

The conversation in the park had started innocently enough—or so it seemed. Quinn was observing Jason carefully while he appeared to carry on a casual conversation. He had partially recognized Jason from the moment that he saw him carrying Victor. The face shown on TV was hard to place, but he knew there was a reward for bringing the kidnapper in, and Quinn needed money.

It was while they talked that Quinn realized that he was more likely to lose money than to cash in on this. He looked at Jason and remembered the comments on the motive for the kidnapping, and there was empathy. Though Quinn was between girlfriends at the moment, he recalled very clearly the gladness he had experienced when his last housemate had come up pregnant. Quinn, of course, was delighted, but she went for an abortion. He finally agreed to take her to the clinic, and the welfare people paid for it. But the relationship was never the same. "I guess I couldn't get over her killing my kid, 'cause everything really went to pot after that," he explained to Jason. He told Jason what had been on his mind and asked if he needed a place to stay.

"Can't understand letting the kid die just because he's got problems," Quinn tried to explain his sudden softness. "It's like picking on little kids."

Once Jason had established his address, he immediately mailed his letter. Quinn didn't require anything of Jason, but Jason felt compelled to at least clean up the place. It wasn't disorderly. Quinn was relatively neat, but things that couldn't be seen were simply not cleaned. While Quinn was at the metal fabrication shop, Jason made the most of cleaning the more public areas of the house—he was hesitant to do anything with Quinn's bedroom.

While Quinn did use drugs—and even occasionally sold some—it was not his daily habit. This puzzled Jason because it seemed so likely that someone of Quinn's background would be heavily involved, but Quinn seemed to stick with smoking an occasional joint and hoisting a couple of beers.

Jason cooked a bachelor goulash for dinner. After the two of them sat down to eat, Jason bowed his head for the blessing. Quinn followed suit.

"Quinn?" Jason asked after the prayer. "You mind if I ask you a personal question?"

"Ask away, Jase. Don't mean you'll get an answer, hu-hu," Quinn retorted.

"It seems to me that a guy like you would be more into drugs and other things," Jason asked. "But you really seem moderate about that stuff. Why?"

Quinn appeared to be considering the question, and a grin broke across his face as he seemed to remember something funny. "Kind of a story," he answered. "It started when my ol' lady and me—the one I had about eight years ago—were in a knock-down-drag-out in the middle of the street. A woman came out of her house and got us to sit in her living room and cool off. This lady and her husband, John and Carol, helped us both see how we were messin' ourselves up with crack and crap like that. They're Christians—I mean *real* Christians. They really helped me. I guess I wouldn't want them to see me strung out again, so I keep it cool on the heavy drugs. I mean, I believe in God and all that, and these people showed me how He must feel about me messin' up. So I stay as straight as I can."

"Then why do you use drugs at all?" Jason asked.

"Well, I s'pose God really don't want me usin' any of the stuff," he answered looking down into his plate. "But I try—I really try—I mean, I believe God is there and that He cares about me—John and Carol showed me that—but I guess I just don't know how to do it right. I wouldn't have any right to say I was a Christian or anything—but I think about God a lot."

•

September 15

Dear Alvin,

You can see my new address. It seems the FBI cranked up their search efforts since our last communication. The baby is OK, and I am staying with someone I met in the park. He recognized me from one of those crime-watch programs and considered turning me in for the reward. But he felt bad about that and gave me and the baby a home instead. He has a real tender spot for the Lord.

Pass my other letter on to Daniella and the kids. The letter that follows was written before I met my benefactor.

My money is OK. But I suspect Daniella's may be running out. Tell her to sell the western albums—she knows who has made offers. I probably won't have any way to hold onto them anyway if the RICO is successful or if I get caught on this.

Sptmawbpwttc.

Jason

Alvin read the other letter before going over to his wall safe and removing Daniella's pregnancy announcement. Quickly, he wrote a short note to Jason and sealed it in a plain envelope which he addressed to the Phoenix house where Jason and the baby stayed. *I'll have someone mail this today,* he thought. But he took warning from Jason's reference to increased FBI surveillance.

When he went to lunch, he passed the envelope to the waitress, a long-time friend and one-time client, and asked her innocently if she would mail it. "Sure," she said and stuffed it in her apron pocket.

●

Jason tiptoed out of his bedroom after a two-hour struggle with Victor's iron will to stay awake and what seemed to be colic. Victor's will had not been victorious. Now he purred softly in his sleep. Jason quietly closed the door and went into the living room. "How about a little chewing gum for the mind," he said aloud to himself as he flipped on the small, rather beat-up looking television and dropped himself in the overstuffed chair covered with a madras-print sheet.

Quinn was not big on television, so his set was a depressing little black-and-white affair that seemed out of place near the well-cared-for component stereo set on the shelves next to it. Quinn really liked music—especially jazz from the early 1960s. He didn't have the patience to discuss the "philosophy" of jazz—he just knew what he liked and bought it.

The little set warmed, and the screen rolled and finally stabilized. Jason was dumbfounded. There on the screen was Daniella. It was the Don Tinnamen talk show, and she was speaking. "If you are implying that Jason has abandoned me and our children," she said looking squarely at Tinnamen, "you are grossly misrepresenting the true situation."

Jason knew that expression on Daniella's face. It denoted her anger—but an anger carefully controlled. She continued, "Jason left because he *loves* people—and particularly his family. He would not have had to leave if this death-dealing culture did not persecute those who defend life. He would do the same for his own children—or *yours*, Mr. Tinnamen. If he didn't, he would not be leaving his own children a world worth inheriting."

Tinnamen blanched and stumbled for words—an uncommon occurrence. Quickly, he turned to the audience. "What do you make of that?" he asked.

A middle-aged woman rose and said, "She has a point. What kind of country are we handing our children when people who try to save lives are chased around like criminals?"

Tinnamen's face soured in obvious disappointment that her comments had placed Jason in a positive light. Jason, watching the scene, felt a thrill of excitement at the point so pungently made.

Dr. Elgin Chapman's voice broke in from the side, and then his face filled the screen. "She keeps saying that Jason cares—but what thought did he give to the agony of the Kellys? The question isn't about saving lives—the question is: who decides?"

"Yes," Daniella called out, "and let's certainly not give the baby a say in it. Why not just strangle him so no one will have to hear him cry?"

"Actually, she has a point," chimed in Dominic Stanford. "This is why Americans for Medical Choice fights for the right of death with dignity—and doctor-assisted deliverance. There is actually no sense making a child suffer without food and water until it dies and spending health care dollars on watching and caring for the child in the intervening days. It is best in hopeless cases like the Kelly Baby to allow for a lethal injection."

Daniella wasted not a second. "That's what I've been trying to say. If we can accept killing a child by starvation, it cannot be very long before someone suggests that it is more 'compassionate' to just snuff them out in the first place if they don't measure up to somebody's standards of perfection. And another thing, Baby Kelly was no 'hopeless case' as Stanford says. He is alive today—and without any extraordinary help—in fact, under severely restricted circumstances where it would be nearly impossible to get medical help if needed."

"But what about the Kellys?" Tinnamen injected.

"What about them? They wanted to kill the child because he is retarded. Jason wanted him—warts and all. Why should they care if someone wants their castoffs—their garbage?"

A swelling "Woo-o-o" came from the crowd, and Daniella, her eyes burning hot, looked at the audience. "What would you recommend? Killing *all* the retarded?"

"She posed the question," Tinnamen said to the group. "What *do* you recommend?"

He held the microphone up to a man in the first row. "I don't know if I would want to live life if they knew I would be severely retarded. I mean, it would have to be a pretty crummy life."

Daniella had heard this before. "First of all, there is no way to tell if the baby will be severely or only mildly retarded. But besides that, who are you to say that someone else's life is so miserable he should be killed? Are you God? A mind reader? If retarded people are so miserable, why do they have a lower suicide rate than so-called normal people? Maybe they know something we don't—like that life is precious? I believe God places ultimate value on all human life—regardless of age, stage, or condition—because they are created in His image."

Reverend Thomas Hillyard spoke up. "Well, the theological question is whether these born with severe abnormality are indeed bearers of the *imago Dei*—the image of God."

Dr. Lasant could not restrain the look of disgust on his face as he said, "Perhaps, then, Reverend Hillyard will volunteer to sit on the committee to pass judgment over who will be certified *imago Dei* ?"

"Well, that's not exactly what I meant—" Hillyard began.

"Oh? Backing out so soon, Reverend Hillyard?" Lasant lampooned. He turned to look at the audience. "Reverend Hillyard is not alone in his unwillingness to actually lay his hands to the task. A small group of justices said killing the unborn was a woman's choice, and now American society repeats and compounds the error by saying that murdering newborns is the parents' decision. Everyone wants to assign responsibility to someone else. In psychology it is called 'denial.' In religious terms it reflects the Biblical assertion that men love darkness rather than light."

Tinnamen just began to answer when the credits rolled, and the volume of the theme music covered the greater part of his comments. He had missed his cue to wrap up with a final statement, and the opportunity was lost. Lasant's final barb was the last word on the subject.

I wish I had seen the whole thing, Jason thought. He knew why he was here with Victor and Daniella was on the TV. *I would never be able to think on my feet that way*, he realized. He then began to feel that singular emptiness created by the distance from his family. But Victor let out a cry, and Jason had no more time for self-pity.

•

Daniella's fierceness gave way after the confrontation. In the hotel that night she cried. Alvin had called to read her the latest note, and she was stunned by Jason's suggestion that she sell the album collection. It wasn't until that moment that Daniella fully realized the possibility of permanent consequences from the whole affair. *This could go on forever*, she thought. She could imagine no scenario with a good ending.

"What's the matter, Mommy?" Monica asked.

"I just miss your Daddy," she replied. "Here, let me brush your hair; then I'll read you and the others a story before bed."

"Aw, bedtime? Already? Can't we stay up and look at the lights?"

Daniella smiled. "Yes, I suppose you can. After all, we don't get to New York every day."

Monica ran out gleefully to tell the others the good news.

11

Harvey Moskowitz sat at the dinner table with his wife, Regina, who made it a habit to have a well-set table, complete with candles, at least once a week. Mostly, she was not one for formalities, but she always felt that such dinners enhanced their marriage—and they did. These special times helped make up for the irregular hours of a special agent. They had had no children, so the china was intact. Both had wanted children, but it simply never happened. Regina was short and somewhat heavy, but she wore an almost constant smile that immediately attracted people.

Tonight Harvey was preoccupied. "What's wrong, Harvey?" Regina finally asked.

Awakening from thought, his hand holding his fork on the plate, he spoke. "It's this Crabb case," he answered. "I *know* he's in Phoenix, but I can't seem to get any Bureau cooperation down there. They say I don't have enough solid indicators. The special agent in charge down there is so totally consumed with some dope ring that he will not 'waste Bureau resources' on finding Crabb."

"You aren't that easily upset, Harvey," she added. "What else?"

Harvey's long face wore a scowl. "The Bureau has put Crabb on low priority—not openly, or anything—but they are starting to load me with trivial jobs. It's just their way of saying, 'It's not important to chase Crabb.' The latest slap was a baby-sitting detail for some political rally."

"A political rally?"

"Yeah," he nodded his head. "It seems that the American Abortion Action Group is taking this Irish doctor and parading him as some kind of abortion rights hero. One of the rallies will be here in Salem. I've got to work on security."

"You mean Sean Jones—the one the Irish are trying to extradite for the death penalty?"

"Aw, that's just media bull-hockey." He saw disapproval in her eyes. She always wanted him to be more refined, particularly when they had their special dinners. "Sorry, honey," he said sincerely. "Anyway, my friends at Immigration tell me that the Irish have never asked for the doctor to be sent back. The Irish government attitude is 'good riddance.' And Ireland doesn't have the death penalty. The whole thing is a mirage cooked up by the abortion groups to hype their issue. Kind of a dirty tactic—but it works, I guess."

"It's hard to believe that the news wouldn't look up facts like the one on the death penalty," Regina said.

Harvey gave her a cynical grin. "Hey, reporters are lazy like everyone else. They do as little digging as they think they need—especially if what they have confirms what they already believe. That's also why they love good sound bites—it saves them having to actually listen to the person they are interviewing. You get used to not believing the press a lot. This Crabb case is a good example. The way the press has presented him—as a dangerous racketeer and kidnapper—is totally inaccurate. He's not a bit dangerous, and he's only a racketeer because people who make their financial and political hay supporting abortion are suing him as such. Anyone can be sued—it doesn't make them some kind of mobster. Crabb's committed a serious crime, all right, and warrants tracking down. But *dangerous*? Not a chance."

"But why would he do what he's doing then?" she asked.

Harvey swallowed the bite of food he had in his mouth and took a sip of wine to clear his throat. "I think the simplest explanation is his religion—just like his wife's been saying all along. Probably thinks of himself like someone hiding Jews from the Nazis or slaves escaping from the South. He really believes he's saved the baby's life."

"Well, did he?" Regina asked.

Harvey had never given that much thought before. He stopped eating and looked off into space for a moment while he stroked his narrow chin. "Yeah," he said. "Yeah, I suppose he did."

•

"Hey, I got a present for ya, Jim," Quinn said, finally getting the hang of calling Jason by his pseudonym. Across the room flew a paper bag that landed flat on the floor with a loud whump!

"What is it?" Jason asked. He opened the bag and pulled out a pair of old license plates.

"My uncle has a van like yours—only a year older," Quinn said as he rooted through the refrigerator for a beer. "It's totaled out, and he's been swappin' parts out of it and will scrap the rest. I got the plates, and he signed over the registration for you—even gave a bill of sale. You can put 'em on your van to cut down visibility—as long as the cops don't check too close."

"Thanks, Quinn," Jason said genuinely.

"No sweat, man. How is the kid, anyway?"

"He's gotten over that fussy streak, but he is sleeping a lot—I hope nothing's wrong."

"Hey, speaking of something wrong," Quinn said, "my car is doing something really weird. Think you could check it out." He picked up the plates and held them up. "You work on your specialty—mechanics, and I'll work on mine—swappin' plates on your van, hu-hu. Here, take my car out around the block—you'll see the problem." Quinn tossed Jason the keys.

Jason looked hesitant.

"I'll watch the little guy. He'll be OK," Quinn assured him.

Jason nodded and minutes later drove off in the battered pickup Quinn called his own.

Soon the limping vehicle returned to its stall. Jason popped the hood and dove beneath it. Shortly afterward, he entered the house wiping his grimy hands on a rag. "Sounds like you may have punched a lifter through a rocker—probably up front—you're really low on oil. That may have caused it. If you have some tools, I could fix it tomorrow—Victor willing," he added as a warning.

Quinn agreed and arranged for Jason to drive him to and from work the next day. When Quinn went out to change the plates on the old van, Jason sat down and pulled out Daniella's letter again. *Pregnant*, he thought to himself. *What a blessing. If only I could be there.* It had been two weeks since he had received the letter, and he was still amazed by the announcement.

•

Alvin dropped the cartridge into the VCR, punched "Play," and waited for the image to come on the screen. The tape had come in an overnight pouch. Suddenly there was a baby on the monitor. A voice-over, obviously Jason, said, "This is Baby Kelly. He has another name which will be revealed when he is safe. As you can see, he is alive and happy. Beside him is a copy of the *New York Times* with today's headline for date verification. I am sending this short tape in case people are worried that he has come to some harm. He would not be alive today had the Kellys been allowed to continue their so-called treatment."

The pictures of the baby continued for another thirty seconds before going to black. There was nothing in the video to indicate where the pictures might have been taken—only the corner of two bare walls and the top of a bed. Certainly, the *Times* could be bought in almost any major city.

Toley looked at the letter from Jason. He had suggested that Alvin make copies for distribution to the media and that one be sent to the Kellys. Alvin thought the idea had merit—but perhaps at a more strategic time.

He put the tape in the safe for the time being.

•

Jason pulled the van up in front of the old Quonset hut that housed the metal fabrication shop. Sparks flew from the arc welders, and blue light flickered eerily on the walls. Everything was coated with a thick black grime—a blend of the oils and grease used to coat and protect new metal and the inevitable dirt and metal filings that were everywhere in the place. Near the door, Quinn was talking with another worker. When he spotted the van, he raised his arm in salute, said a few more words to his friend, and trotted over.

Quinn swung wide the door and first greeted Victor before hopping into his seat. "Hey, man," he said, "I gotta make a stop on the way home, OK?"

"Just point the way," Jason answered.

"Hang a right when you pull out. I gotta stop at this guy's house and get some tools he borrowed from me. You'll have to stay in the van and wait—the guy don't like new people—a dealer, y'know. But don't worry, I'm not getting any dope. I wouldn't do that to you guys—bring dope into your car."

Jason looked askance, but reluctantly agreed. After following Quinn's directions for several miles, Jason pulled the van to the curb. "It's around the corner. I'll be back in a minute," Quinn said as he slammed the door shut.

About ten minutes after Quinn had disappeared, Jason looked up from his Bible in surprise. Outside, he heard the tac-tac of semi-automatic rifle fire. He had heard it before at a ranch owned by a friend of his who was also a gun collector.

"Take it easy, Victor," he said to the sleeping figure. Jason started the motor and rolled the van toward the corner. He knew what was happening as soon as he was able to see down the street. Men and cars were scattered in front of a small brick house with a chain-link fence. The men all wore dark blue vests emblazoned with FBI or PPD. He could see Quinn seated behind an unmarked, though obviously official, car with his hands curiously pinned behind him. A man with PPD on his vest squatted beside him with a pistol held in ready position as he peered across the trunk of the car toward the house.

The tac-tac came again, and the men in the vests all hit

cover. A car windshield shattered, and three FBI men made a dash for the side of the house. Jason had no desire to watch the scenario play out. Quinn was under arrest, and there was no telling where that would lead. He had to force himself to round the corner away from the scene at a moderate speed.

In the rearview mirror, Jason could see Quinn seated on the street. "I know he'll understand," Jason said to himself uncertainly.

Returning to Quinn's house, Jason quickly rounded up his and Victor's belongings and tried to remove all traces of their stay there. As he left the building, he taped a note on the front door.

> Quinn,
>
> Thanx for everything.
>
> J

This note could mean anything. "J" could be a man or woman. Its placement on the outside would indicate that the writer may not have had access to the house. He could only hope that he had swept the house clean of his and Victor's presence. The bed they had used was folded up again and the blankets put in the linen closet; the diapers were taken from the laundry room—and even the special diaper solution was removed.

Jason checked his cash reserves. He was sufficiently endowed that he felt no anxiety.

Victor was awake again, but placid as they began their trip. Before Jason turned onto the northbound highway 17, he jotted a quick note for Alvin.

October 6

Alvin,

There has been some trouble, and I must move again. Everyone is fine. The money is holding out well. I'll be in touch as soon as I land. Give Daniella and the kids—especially whosit—my love.

Vcwtomtbrtohtoab.

Jason

Jason dropped the letter in the mail slot and aimed his van toward the highway. In a few hours he was driving in the dark through Flagstaff. The bitter winds of impending winter stripped through the thin coats of the few souls to be seen on its wooden sidewalks. Thus far, fall had been dry, and there was yet no real snow on the ground. It would have been a relief to the eye if there had been. A small motel loomed ahead. Jason decided to stop. The driving had been tedious, but the frequent stops to tend to Victor were draining as well. *Now I know why God made parents in pairs,* he thought as he fell into the motel bed exhausted.

•

"Hey, I was just going there to get my tools, man," Quinn said calmly.

"Yeah, right, Quinten—is that right? Quinten?" the detective asked.

Quinn flushed. "Yeah, but they call me Quinn, OK?"

"Well, if it is only tools you were after, I don't suppose you would mind giving permission for a search on your house?" asked the heavy, perspiring detective, pushing up his shirt sleeves.

Quinn thought of Jason and Victor. He was sure they had headed back to the house and probably packed and left. *Need to give them as much time as possible.* "Nah, I don't think so," he replied.

"We can just get a warrant, Quinn," the detective reminded.

"So, get one," came Quinn's rejoinder. *That ought to give them a few hours.*

12

The fax machine spewed out a ream of paper, and Harvey Moskowitz picked it up and began scanning it. It was a report of what had been found at the Quinten Roberts house in Phoenix. An especially alert special agent had spotted an oddity during the drug search—a can of baby formula in the refrigerator—and he remembered the bulletin about Baby Kelly. His curiosity aroused, he spoke with his squad supervisor who obtained a search warrant specifying the Baby Kelly case.

Jason did a pretty good sweep, Harvey admitted to himself. *But not good enough.* The formula container was being run on the fingerprint-scanner through the Oregon State Police. The results were due soon. Best of all, however, was the letter from "Alvin," whom Harvey assumed was Alvin Toley. The sheet of paper had apparently slipped behind the dresser, escaping Jason's notice. Harvey studied the odd combination of letters in the last line of the note. *Some kind of verification code,* he added to his mental notes. *Too bad we only have one. It will make it hard to decipher.*

Another solid piece was the note found on the front door. The scrawl clearly matched Jason's nearly illegible writing, and the characteristic use of "Thanx" with the "x" matched other writing samples Harvey had obtained.

We're getting closer to you, Crabb, Harvey thought, his jaw muscles tightening. *We'll get you yet.* Harvey knew that sudden flights by fugitives often left more clues as there was less time for planning. He hoped more of these would begin to surface.

Moskowitz faxed a copy of the note to Washington and requested a cryptography examination of the strange letter sequence. Already, he had obtained various wiretap permits on the family and the lawyer, but the quarry were cagy, and these had turned up nothing so far. Yet even though he could only afford the minimum of monitoring, he felt there was some purpose served. Harvey believed they were aware of the wiretap possibility, and that alone constricted their activities and might lead them to crucial errors.

A newsman from *The Sun* had been hounding him for any breaks in the case. Was it time to leak this to the media? As he pondered, suddenly he had an inspiration.

He picked up the phone receiver and tapped in the number for *The Sun.*

"Hello, John? Moskowitz, FBI."

•

Alvin leaned back in his chair at the defense table waiting for the bailiff's "All rise." The jury for this civil suit was apparently confirmed in their verdict, and it was only a matter of time before this final phase would be finished. He was confident his client would be released from the suit.

From behind him came his "go-fer," Jim Ellis, a tall blond football player-type who went to Willamette University sometimes and worked odd jobs for Toley. "Hey,

Al," he whispered, "something's up on the Crabb case; there are reporters waiting outside to ambush you after this verdict. You want me to run interference?"

"Nope," he replied. "I've been expecting them. Got a tip from inside *The Sun*—someone from advertising—and I've got a surprise for them." He patted his huge briefcase and smiled knowingly at Ellis.

A movement in the corner of the courtroom and the bailiff's call signaled the resumption of the case. The judge nodded to the attorneys, and they were seated. The jury filed in. The foreman announced that Alvin's client, owner of a small bookstore, had not been liable for the injury sustained by a customer who had just left his shop. Alvin smiled and nodded to his client who collapsed in his chair with relief.

"Boy," the client said, "I was worried there for a while."

Alvin returned, "It was a pretty straightforward case. If the judge followed the law and the jury listened at all, it was almost a sure thing. Just be grateful you are not a pro-lifer on trial. They'd have strung you up by your thumbs."

Alvin stashed the remainder of his paperwork in his smaller briefcase, snapped it shut, and headed toward the door.

Outside waited several reporters. When he emerged, their eyes brightened—the predator spotting the prey. "What do you have to say about Jason Crabb nearly being picked up in a big drug bust in Arizona? What is he doing involved in a drug ring—and does he still have the baby?"

Alvin set his briefcases down on a bench and held up his hands palms out. "Hold it a minute. First, if Jason has associated with drug dealers, it is only because law enforcement has forced him underground where these people are in abundance. I can assure you that Jason does not take or sell drugs. No one—including me—has a lot of details on what happened in Phoenix. As to the baby, I can assure you that he is alive and happy—neither of which would be true if he had completed the course of 'treatment' at St. Luke's—and I can demonstrate that for you."

Alvin popped open the large briefcase to reveal a half-dozen video cassettes. He took several out and distributed one to each media representative. "You'll find a recent short clip featuring Baby Kelly on there," he added. "As you view it, remember that this little guy would be dead if it weren't for Jason Crabb."

He closed the briefcase, hoisted it, and strode down the hall.

•

These were long days on the road for Jason and Victor. Fortunately the old Ford van had an excellent heater. The blistering cold outside and the skifts of snow they ran across at the higher elevations in the Rockies felt more like winter than fall. Victor seemed to be cranky the whole time—at least when he was awake. This forced Jason to stop often and hold him or play with him when he could no longer bear Victor's complaints. It made the going slow.

It occurred to Jason that the air pressure difference in the mountains might be making Victor's ears uncomfortable— but he could do little to remedy that. His best option was to pass through Denver and head east toward the flat country of Kansas. Snowstorms seemed to follow him through the mountain passes. He heard local weather reports on the radio.

It took him five days to reach Denver. The mighty mountains seemed to drop to nothing at the edges of the city. He stayed in a squalid little motel for a couple of nights before continuing east on Interstate 70. Gradually descending flatlands spread before them. Denver was the beginning of a long downhill roll toward the great plains.

Jason pointed the van toward Kansas and drove.

●

Quinn had not talked much. He claimed he thought "Jim" was only a poor homeless man with a kid. He had never, he said, even gotten the guy's last name.

The detectives didn't believe him, but what could they do? There was no evidence to link him with the Baby Kelly kidnapping.

Quinn had, however, given them the name Baby Kelly was using. He could think of no plausible reason not to have known Victor's name.

●

The flatness of the Kansas farm country threatened to hypnotize Jason. There was nothing for miles but vast stubbled fields and an occasional farmhouse with outbuildings. The openness made him feel alone and vulnerable. He was grateful when the sun went down on the vast expanse so he couldn't see it any more. Many access roads led off into the endless fields. When he finally tired, he exited the Interstate and ducked the van into one of these to deal with the fussy Victor.

There's no telling how far we are from the next motel, Jason thought as he pinned a clean diaper on the struggling Victor. He noted how quickly Victor had developed since the exercise regimen had begun. The baby was nearly able to roll over by himself. Jason knew he must take extra care now when he laid Victor down anywhere so that his first roll would not be off the end of a bed or couch.

Jason yawned as he completed his task. He felt a weariness in his body that the adrenaline alertness of driving had masked. He knew it would be foolhardy to go any further. He would just spend the night here in the turnout. "Now, Victor," he said, "you must cooperate—there's a new word for you—*cooperate*."

Victor seemed to understand and dropped off slightly more quickly than Jason. Soon both were breathing softly under a heavy down quilt that had been a gift from Dorothy Thompson in California. She found it virtually useless in the warm weather there. But her mother had given it to her when Dorothy moved "out west" where her mother envisioned her sleeping under covered wagons in the high Sierras.

Both bodies were warmly tucked under the billowing blanket when Jason awoke to a tapping sound. Cautiously he peeked out from under the massive cover into the biting chill of the van's interior. At the frosty windshield was a silhouette of a man wearing a baseball cap. He was saying something unclear to Jason's sleep-fuzzed mind. "Just a minute," Jason called. The tapping stopped.

Jason carefully extricated himself from under the blanket so as not to expose Victor to the cold. With remarkable agility, he moved up to the passenger seat and rolled down the window. "Yes?" he asked.

"Blockin' my road, son," the old farmer said without malice. "Need to get some materials into this field, and you're in m'way." The farmer wore a heavy denim coat with a horse blanket lining and the stereotypical John Deere cap on his head. He was short and wiry, and the wrinkles on his face seemed etched in by cold winds and baked on by blistering heat waves. But there was no meanness in his face or his eyes.

"Oh, sorry, Mister," Jason responded automatically. "I just couldn't drive further last night. Hope you don't mind my using your turnout."

"Not at all, son. In fact, if you're needing breakfast, my wife should be finishing it up in just a bit. Soon as I drop this stuff off, I'll be back, and you can follow me. There's not a good place to eat for quite a ways, you know."

"Well, I—" Jason began, but the farmer had already turned back to his truck. Jason slid over to the driver's seat and fired up the engine. The farmer soon was driving down the access road. Jason looked at his watch, which read 5:30.

Jason groaned, "Five-thirty? I wonder if even God is up yet."

As promised, the farmer was only gone a short time. Jason dressed more appropriately and brushed his teeth using the cold water from a canteen. He checked and changed Victor and bundled him in a thick bunting. Formula was another matter, as he felt it was too cold for the tyke. Victor was not happy about this and began to demand his breakfast. Jason began to put Victor through his exercises to pass the time, but this upset Victor more. Just as Jason put Victor into the seat and the inside of the van was beginning to warm, he saw the old farmer's truck returning from the chores. By this time the frost on the windshield had cleared sufficiently for Jason to peer out through an area the size of a thirteen-inch television screen. He threw the transmission into "drive" and followed as the truck passed without slowing.

Almost a mile down the road stood a small clapboard house on the right. The bleak morning light could not reveal its color. The truck pulled into a graveled roadway that led to the farmyard; Jason followed. Still unhappy, Victor squawked and called out. Assorted outbuildings stood around the edges of the yard, and an inviting, warm yellow glow showed through the white bird's-eye curtains where Jason assumed the kitchen must be. The chimney emitted a small stream of white smoke. The house needed a paint job—badly—but everything about it evoked the word *home*. Jason prayed that they would not be recognized.

•

Sue Curran was plump, mostly white-haired, and in her late fifties. She bustled around the kitchen with amazing efficiency producing a platter of eggs and another of flapjacks. She had also taken over the care and feeding of Victor who now rested contentedly in the crook of her arm swigging away on his bottle. He was like a natural extension of her body as she swirled through the room keeping track of the frying and toasting food.

Her husband Pat quietly ate his breakfast and observed Jason, who watched Sue in amazement.

"Where could you possibly be going with such a little one, I'm asking myself," she said into the air. But Jason knew he would have to have an answer—and soon.

Sue stopped momentarily and hoisted Victor higher to nuzzle his face. Not long after, she finished her kitchen dance and sat down beside Jason urging him to eat. He needed little encouragement.

Sue and Pat waited patiently as Jason ate; then the grilling began. Sue took up from where she had left off—the question thrown into the air. Sedated with home cooking, Jason was defenseless against her motherly inquisition. Soon she had plied the entire truth from his lips. *I hope the FBI doesn't have one of these,* thought Jason during the questioning.

The Currans had heard about Baby Kelly, of course, and sympathized with the baby's plight. They had seen through the media fog to the facts of the case—Victor's life. "Used to looking at the roots of things 'round here," Pat said as he re-lit his pipe. "Got no use for packages that are more important than contents."

Sue sat to the side holding the sleeping bundle. "Such a quiet baby," she noted.

Jason turned to her. "He is, but that can be a problem for Down's babies. They sleep away and don't get their exercise and don't learn to control their bodies. I often have to wake him for his exercises. He doesn't like it, but I have already seen progress in his development."

Pat puffed several times on the pipe to keep it going and asked, "What're your plans, son? You gonna just keep running, or what?"

"Well," Jason answered, "up to now, I've concentrated on just staying lost in the crowd—so to speak—but the heat has been turned up, and it seems the FBI has some leads on me. But I haven't had a chance to really think of any kind of long-term solution to this."

Sue added, "This place is as safe as any. Maybe he could stay here, Pat, until he thinks of something? He could use Patty's old room."

Pat mused over her suggestion for a moment. Jason felt the anxiety rise. Suddenly, Pat nodded. "I suppose he could, Ma. Suppose he could."

13

Watching for a tail, Alvin had taken a circuitous route to church. When he was sure it was safe, he quickly dropped the letter in the mailbox and drove toward the old brick building. Inside the envelope were instructions for Jason to memorize the new "drop" address. Alvin's other friend was beginning to feel antsy about the possibility of the FBI paying an unexpected and dreaded call. Alvin understood and located a new post for Jason's mail. *Probably a good idea to change anyhow,* he thought.

The last place Alvin had expected Jason to land was Kansas—on a farm, no less. Here it was, a week before Thanksgiving, and there was no letup in the relentless manhunt. Of course, Jason had to be very careful what he wrote in his letters so as not to give away his location or his benefactors. Alvin destroyed letters and envelopes immediately and completely. He kept only copies of Jason's correspondence so there was little direct evidence to be sifted through. About the time when he wondered if he were becoming too paranoid, some indication of a phone tap or other investigative work would surface. "Just because I'm paranoid," he would remind himself, "doesn't mean no one's out to get me."

Jason indicated that he was seeking a permanent resolution to his situation, but that he had yet to find any alternatives to his fugitive status.

Alvin had watched in wonder as Daniella cheerfully did the pregnancy duck-walk across the sanctuary at church last Sunday. The support for Jason had grown thin, and voices of dissent about his "crime" had begun to rise from the congregation. Yet Daniella never wavered. Pastor Elkins was betwixt and between and—though he believed in what Jason had done—felt it was most important to maintain "unity." So he said little publicly except to try to sooth the clucking tongues of Jason's detractors.

The pressure Pastor Elkins felt was more than just social. New legal theories of church liability promoted in seminars by the American Legal Society suggested that individual church members could be held financially liable if their church were shown to be guilty of some tort complaint. He had heard rumors that the RICO suit that included Jason might be expanded to include the church. Alvin explained the theory to the pastor saying, "The idea is that Jason claims his pro-life work—and now the situation with Baby Kelly—is essentially a religious act. Since he gets his religious instruction here, the plaintiffs may assert that the church and its members are at least partly liable. I know the idea stretches credulity, but with the way the courts have been going lately . . ." Alvin shrugged.

"Not very reassuring," Elkins replied.

"You need to know, Pastor," he said, "this same thing could happen if someone just picketed a clinic or became visible in any kind of pro-family work that offends the social order. What can I say? Jesus never said being a

Christian would be safe. If it's any comfort, I'll take on the church *pro bono*—if it comes to that."

"Well, that's good," said Elkins cautiously, "but a lot of members of the congregation are worried that their own assets are on the line. Some have even suggested we publicly excommunicate Jason—distance ourselves from him."

"A lot of members?" Alvin queried, knowing church politics. "Or just a few squeaky wheels? Pastor, the point here is what is *right* —not what causes the fewest waves. Christ never called us to apathy—nor did He call us to pluralism and majority rule, or Noah would never have built the boat, Moses would have died at birth, and Elijah would have gone to work for Ahab and Jezebel. This is not the time to waver on what is right—and you know Jason is right."

•

Harvey Moskowitz looked down at the materials spread out on his desk and shook his head slowly. *For all the apparent leads in Phoenix*, he thought, *Crabb seems to have vanished*. Moskowitz was rarely fooled by appearances. He knew that spurts of evidence could come in—only to lead nowhere.

A thin lead indicated that Jason and the baby had headed toward Denver, but the information was tenuous. Harvey felt stymied. His only hope was to convince the special agent in charge in Denver to put some higher priority on this—despite the fact that the Bureau had reduced its rating.

The more the Bureau tended to let go of the Baby Kelly case, the more Moskowitz was challenged by it. *Amazing*, he thought. *Amazing how a simple mechanic can outwit the entire Bureau for so long.*

Harvey reached across the desk for the phone and dialed Denver.

•

"There's not much to do round here this time of year," Pat said to Jason from under the combine, "so I just do repairs on the machinery and lube it up for spring."

"I'm sure I can help with some of that," Jason answered. "I'm a good mechanic."

"Well, tractor over there could use a rebuild. Know anything about diesel?"

"Some. If you've got a book on it, I can do anything," he said.

"Soon as I get done here we'll go inside," Pat said. "You can start tearing that down tomorrow."

The wiry old farmer pulled himself out from under the machine and dusted himself off. They headed back to the house where Sue was mending a quilt while listening to the low drone of a newscaster on the TV. Victor was rocking on his belly, gnawing contentedly on a green plastic cube.

"It wasn't long ago he didn't have the coordination to do that," Jason said with a hint of pride.

Sue bit off the excess thread and looked up at him. "You've done a good job, Jason," she said.

The newscast switched over to a heated debate. The Irish ambassador, Michael McAuliff, was speaking. "I'll say it again. *We have no death penalty*. We are proud of our defense of life. Dr. Jones would—had he stayed in Ireland— have been charged under the 1867 Offenses Against the Person Act. His offense is serious, but we have never sought extradition—and probably never will. The weekly demonstrations outside the embassy are of no consequence to us—

though the bomb threats have concerned us. I suspect that all the demonstrations are staged just to strengthen the abortion groups here in the States, nothing more."

Betsy Winkler wrinkled her nose and spat out, "Proud of your defense of life? You don't seem to care if women die from back-alley abortions."

"Certainly we do," McAuliff answered, brushing the white hair from his eyes. "We offer them all the help we have, but any woman foolish enough to hire a butcher to do the work of a surgeon should expect trouble. Are you implying that your 'courageous Dr. Jones' was providing unsafe abortions since his abortions were technically 'back-alley?' If so, why do you see him as helping women?"

"If it weren't for your backward and barbaric laws, Mr. McAuliff . . . "

"Backward and barbaric?" he asked. "What do you call dismembering helpless babies, Ms. Winkler? Civilized?"

"And what do you call hounding a man like Dr. Jones and trying to drag him back in irons? I simply don't believe your denials of extradition—I have sources that say you are."

The scene returned to the news reader. "McAuliff is right about one thing," Sue commented. "The pro-abortion crowd is just using this whole thing to stir things up and raise funds." She looked disgusted and pressed the stud on the remote control. The television flicked off.

•

"Sue," Jason called from the doorway, holding Victor high on his shoulder, "where did you get this poem in the bedroom?"

"Oh, you mean the sampler?" she said rising from her

chair. "I made that years ago. It was Patty's favorite—so we moved it from the front room to his bedroom." Sue walked to the bedroom, plucked the framed needlework off the wall, and looked at it longingly. It read,

I see His blood upon the rose,
And in the stars, the glory of His eyes.
His body gleams amid eternal snows.
His tears fall from the skies.

I see His face in every flower;
The thunder and the singing of the birds
Are but His voice—and carven by His power,
Rocks are His written words.

All pathways by His feet are worn;
His strong heart stirs the ever-beating sea;
His crown of thorns is twined by every thorn;
His cross is every tree.

Joseph M. Plunkett (1887–1916)

"He always said it showed how the world's ugliest things—like the cross of Christ—could be for the good, how God could bring great good out of great evil," she added as her eyes glistened with wetness. "The poem was written by an Irish believer while he was imprisoned for his faith. He even saw God's terrible price for us in the beautiful things of the earth. I guess it made his own imprisonment easier when he thought of it as sharing in the suffering of Christ."

"That's the way Paul felt," Jason said.

"Yes, and Patty was always looking to help anyone less fortunate."

Jason looked at the kindly face of Sue Curran as she lifted Victor from his shoulder to cradle him herself. "He comes by that trait honestly," he said. "Watching the way you have taken to doing Victor's exercises and looking after him as if he were your own."

"Well, his daddy has been working on the old tractor, now hasn't he," she said looking closely into Victor's face. Victor grinned widely and let out a giggle. "Yes, and he has lots of fun with Grandma Sue, huh?"

"It's more than that though," Jason said. "I mean, you really didn't have to order that book on raising a Down's baby—and then to actually put it into practice."

"It's no less than I should do for all God's goodness to me. Besides, I've learned so much that I was ignorant of before. For instance, did you know why Down's syndrome used to be called mongolism? It was based on the theory that— because of the shape of the eyes in Down's—these children were evolutionary throwbacks to what they considered a lesser race—the Mongoloids. Talk about scientific racism . . . of course, Dr. Down, the theorist on the syndrome, knew nothing of chromosomes—much less the extra one Victor has. The doctor's belief was the result of the evolutionary theory. But that's the trouble with scientists who don't believe in God. When they don't know something, they presume—and they presume from a godless mentality."

"It's strange," Jason remarked, "that the scientists who believe in evolution are the ones that have classified people as races, but God said He has made us all 'of one blood.' Yet, it is the evolutionist, scientific types that tend to label the Bible as a racist book."

"I've read that assumptions about evolution have actually prevented medical advancement in many ways," Sue said. "They taught for many years that the tonsils and the appendix were useless leftovers from our evolutionary past and could be removed without consequence, but only recently someone discovered that God hasn't made useless spare parts. Both turned out to be important in fighting disease. All this because they wouldn't examine their basic assumptions of evolution."

Jason thought for a moment. "Maybe they thought that the idea of useless parts would disprove God because it would show Him to be a bad designer."

"I suppose," Sue answered. "But a look at Victor's situation tells me we haven't advanced much since Dr. Down in the late 1800s. Obviously, Victor is regarded as 'not fully human' by both society and his parents. It seems even his parents think of him as proof of bad design. I think people who are handicapped are here to show us what *we* are made of. God not only made no useless parts; He made no useless people."

"It's sad," Jason agreed. "I look at Victor and I see God's image—and a reminder of the helpless souls for whom Christ died. It's very much like that poem of yours. This baby reminds me of the great cost God paid for us."

The conversation was suddenly interrupted by the loud blasts that so often accompanied Victor's work on his diapers. Sue and Jason looked at the relieved smile on Victor's face, then at one another. "A fitting end to the philosophy class," Sue said. Both broke into laughter.

"What's so funny?" Pat asked walking into the room.

Again they looked at each other and laughed harder.

Pat shrugged and went on into his bedroom to change. Jason and Sue worked together on the diaper change, and soon Victor was looking for something to fill his mouth. Sue moved toward the kitchen for a bottle and some rice cereal. Jason carried Victor behind her.

"Sue, what happened to Patty?" Jason asked carefully.

"He was a Marine," Sue answered as she stopped stirring

the cereal. "And a good one. He just happened to be in Lebanon when there were a lot of terrorist attacks. He really loved those war-wracked people and planned to go back as a mission worker after his tour of duty was up."

"I'm sorry," Jason said impotently.

Sue was quiet for a moment. Then she spoke softly, "I'm not sure how, but it is like the poem—God can bring great good from great evil."

After feeding Victor, Sue seemed to want to be alone. Jason took Victor back to Patty's old room.

Something about the poem was churning in his mind. It was like there were ideas, plans, and connections being stirred in a furious vortex. But when Jason tried to pin down what was emerging, it slipped like quicksilver from his grasp. "Lord Jesus," he prayed, "if there is something I need to know, please show it to me. But keep me from making mistakes."

14

Daniella sat on the floor with Richard. Before them, the *Ray's Arithmetic* lay open. Pointing at the page, she said, "You must remember to keep the columns straight, or you will lose track and get the wrong answer. Remember, neatness counts—especially in math."

Richard leaned over his paper and continued his work. With some difficulty, Daniella arose and did a pregnant waddle back to the kitchen where Monica was helping her measure flour for the cake they were baking. "Will Dad get back for Christmas, Mom?" Monica's squeaky voice asked.

"I don't know, Monica. We can pray for that."

"Can we keep the baby that he has?" she asked again.

"I hope so. Now measure another cup of flour for me."

"OK. Why does Dad have to be gone so long?"

"Sometimes people have to do God's work even when it's hard, Monica. This is hard for Dad too, and we have to do our hard part by praying and waiting."

"Can we have a puppy for Christmas?"

"Puppies!" exclaimed the tiny voice of Nicole from the kitchen doorway.

Daniella continued her mixing. "We'll have to wait until we can ask your dad about puppies, girls."

The doorbell sounded, and Daniella called to Richard to answer it. "It's Mr. Toley, Mom."

"Hello, Alvin," Daniella called.

Alvin appeared in the doorway behind the now-seated Nicole. "Got another letter from Jason," he said, "and I dropped off a deposit into your account. There are some really faithful people out there supporting you."

"They wouldn't have been there without your talent for fund-raising, Alvin," Daniella replied. "Let me wash my hands, and I'll take that letter."

At the word *letter*, the children gathered around Daniella and formed a train behind her as she walked to the over-stuffed chair and sat down. Even toddling little Jimbo knew enough to get in on the action—especially when Mommy was at the center of it.

Daniella scanned the letter quickly and read aloud those parts that were pertinent to little ears. Alvin stood by.

After the reading, Daniella reassigned Richard to his schoolwork and sent off the little ones to play.

"What is this about an idea he has, Alvin?" she asked.

Alvin shook his head slowly. "I don't have a clue. He didn't say anything more to me than he did to you. It's smart of him not to put it in writing because we have no idea whether our communications security is compromised. That's very frustrating for all of us."

•

"I really appreciate your willingness to watch Victor for a few days," Jason said to Sue.

Sue held the squirmy bundle. "No problem, Jason.

There's not much doing on a farm this time of year anyway. And after all the help you've been on that old tractor, well . . . besides, I like Victor." She turned her face to his and added, "And he likes me, doesn't he?"

Victor let out a squeal and a cackle.

"Here's the address and number I'll be at in Wichita, OK?" he said pinning the scrawled note on the kitchen board. "I think this guy can verify my idea for a resolution to this mess."

Pat grumbled, "Wish you'd tell us what it is."

Jason looked frustrated. "I wish I could too, but the fewer people who know, the better."

"You sure you can trust this fella' in Wichita?" Pat queried.

"As sure as I can be, under the circumstances. I met him a couple of years ago under favorable conditions, and he's more or less an expert in some of the legal questions I have. I need good information, and he can give it, but I don't want to talk on the phone and leave a trail back to here."

With that Jason hefted his duffel bag and headed for the van. He felt a strange emptiness as he walked out. He noted that it was more than just empty arms.

The trip itself was not very long, but Jason met with Jack Thompson for three days. After many hours of computer communications and phone calls, Thompson finally turned to Jason and said, "Technically, you and the kid have a case, Jason, but political realities are another thing altogether. You could try the idea. It has about a fifty/fifty chance— maybe a little better due to the unusual events lately—but you'll have to hurry while the heat's still on."

Jason understood, thanked his friend, and packed his grip again. He would waste no time. He missed Victor, and he was sure of his next step. A call from a pay phone insured that the Currans would have things ready for his arrival.

Just outside of the Wichita city limits, Jason noticed smoke billowing skyward from the road ahead. As he drew closer, he saw twisted metal and glass everywhere and the smoking remains of two vehicles. It looked as though a pickup had attempted to move to the slower lane and struck the side and front of a late model sedan. People were emerging from the ruins as Jason approached. He pulled the van to the emergency lane, grabbed a handful of flares, and headed back to the site almost without hesitation.

He ran by the twisted steel mass, placed a flare about twenty-five yards behind the pile-up, and added another four flares on his way back to the wreck. He ducked his head inside the sedan and saw an older woman still belted into her seat. She looked alert but unable to get out. "Someone will help you out in a moment," he said.

The driver's side was empty except for the expended balloon of the safety air-bag. Apparently, the driver had struggled through the window. Jason saw an older man talking to the driver of the pickup. The man held his head and swayed unsteadily.

Jason hurried over and asked him to lie down as he appeared to be going into shock. The man began to deny it, and then suddenly he collapsed. Jason and the other driver caught him and lowered him to the pavement.

Jason went for some blankets from the van. He covered the elderly man and placed a folded blanket under his feet.

In a few minutes the state patrol appeared on the scene. Suddenly the pickup driver became very nervous. Jason assumed it was because he feared being found at fault.

Another squad car pulled up to assist the first two officers. In the rear of this patrol vehicle was a police dog.

Suddenly, the dog began to paw at the window and howl. The handler looked quizzically at the animal. "All right, Ranger, what is it?" He opened the door. The dog bolted from the seat as if shot from a gun and headed directly for the damaged black pickup truck.

At that, the pickup driver lunged off into the darkness. In the rear of the truck the officers discovered a suitcase with several kilos of cocaine. The wreck had broken the packaging open, and a small sprinkle of the dust had been thrown across the truck bed.

Moments later the place was swarming with ambulances, police vehicles, and press people. The situation looked well in hand, and Jason wanted no questions, so he slipped hurriedly away before there was any organization to the madness.

•

The morning was quiet in Harvey Moskowitz's office, but a damp draft caught him in the back, and he searched out the errant flow of air before settling back to scan the *New York Times*. He looked forward to this daily ritual. It gave him a feel for the current mind-set of the East Coast crowd and thus helped him get a handle on some agency decisions. For instance, noting the reaction in the *Times* to the Presidential Commission on Pornography had enabled him to predict—and thus precede—the agency fad on catching child pornographers.

The fad soon wore out—but not with Harvey. He had always had it in for perverts—especially those who hurt children.

As he came to page 4, something stopped him. He could not actually pin down what it was, but something caught his attention in the photo of a Kansas drug haul. Alarms and sirens went off in Harvey's mind as he carefully read the story.

It seemed that a highway accident north of Wichita had involved a pickup bearing cocaine. The driver had disappeared into the darkness and was yet to be apprehended—but it was the picture that bothered Harvey.

He reached into the center drawer of his oak desk for a pair of scissors, snipped the picture and article from the paper, and clipped it over the picture of his wife on the desk. *Sorry, Hon,* he thought. *I'll figure out what's wrong with this picture yet.*

Methodically, Harvey finished his scan of the *Times*. *I think the next wave may be a return of keen interest in hate crimes*, he thought as he put down the paper. There had been three articles on hate crimes today—all back-East events—and the weeks before had seen more than a smattering of the same.

"Well, I'll be," he said aloud. Harvey set the paper aside and pulled the clipping to him. There he was—kneeling beside a prone figure—Jason Crabb. Crabb was a little hard to distinguish, and he was behind the truck, but Harvey was certain.

He lifted the phone. "Get me Kansas State Police," he ordered. Just then another agent entered the office. Harvey cupped his hand over the receiver and signaled to him. "Tom, get me the Crabb file, please."

•

Jason loaded the last of his and Victor's belongings into the van.

"I wish you would stay for another couple of days. It

looks as if Victor may be coming down with something," Sue said.

Jason absently rubbed his chin. "I wish I could too," he answered. "But I feel as if I had better take this open door now, or it may shut on us. If everything goes well, you should know about the plan in a few days. Just watch the news and—as they say in the fairy tales, 'All will be revealed!'"

"And if it doesn't work?" Sue asked.

"Then you'll hear about that too."

15

The cold was a palpable presence even inside the van. Chicago's infamous wind conspired to steal the warmth from the vehicle's struggling heater almost before it entered the air. Jason's breath was visible before him as he drove down Uptown area streets in search of a particular address. City grime stained the winter whiteness that hid all the buildings in a sameness that numbed the mind. Wind-driven sludge and sticky flakes obscured even the street signs as he watched for the building.

Thank God, Victor sleeps through stuff like this, Jason reminded himself, glancing over at the softly breathing bundle. Victor was wrapped up in a snowsuit and a bunting. A blanket formed a tent over his head to trap the heat of his breath near his face. Jason worried that it might not be enough.

Ahead, Jason saw the sign—AJF—American Jesus Freaks. The AJF was a unique outgrowth of the late '60s youth revival—but it was far more than a collection of aging hippies-gone-Christian or a latent flame of liberal politics mixed with salvation. Eclectic was perhaps the best description of the hard-working people who shared life in the former warehouse and who provided an incredible array of human services to the surrounding decaying neighborhood. They ministered the gospel accompanied by sweat to the many needs there—from painting a shut-in's dingy apartment to giving band concerts for the neighbors. They had an open invitation in their publications to "drop in." Jason was about to do that. He had arranged a flight out of O'Hare at a travel agency a couple of days ago as he drove through Des Moines. His flight was not due to leave for three more days, and he hoped AJF would not be too prone to ask questions. His money was running low after paying cash for the flight, and staying at a Chicago hotel would eat up the rest of his reserves. He hoped to hold onto a thousand dollars in case his ploy failed when he reached his destination.

The brakes squealed as he pulled up in front of the old brick building. "Well, here goes, little," he said aloud to Victor. He carefully lifted the baby, kicked open the van door, and admitted an icy blast. Soon he had shouldered his way into the moderately warm foyer of the building. Victor was stirring in Jason's arms, and Jason was unsure of where to go. On the right was a set of stairs leading to the next story; on the left a hallway disappeared around the corner. There were no signs, and the interior smelled of fresh paint.

A noise on the stairs made Jason turn, and he saw a lanky man in his early twenties loping down. "Thought I heard someone," the long-haired man said. "Just painted, so the signs are down. Come on with me." He headed back up the stairs with Jason following.

The young man called back, "I'm Ruff—that's R-U-F-F— Ruff. Looks like you might need some help—I'll show you where you can stow that bundle."

Just then, Victor let out a questioning call that might have been translated, "Where am I?"

Ruff turned and looked wide-eyed at Jason. "On second thought, maybe we better find some other arrangement for your 'bundle.'"

Ruff reached down and pulled back the blanket to reveal Victor's unhappy face. "Let's go see my wife, uh—what's your name?"

"Jim," Jason answered. "Jim Cramer. And this is Victor."

"It's getting late, Jim. We'll put you two up with us tonight and go see the elders tomorrow, OK?"

"Sounds good to me," Jason replied with some relief.

●

Special agents in Kansas came up empty at first, but someone remembered Jason's plates. Harvey Moskowitz drove the investigators by long-distance phone calls until it was established that the plates belonged to an Arizona van—a van that belonged to a relative of none other than Quinten Roberts. *A little too much coincidence,* Harvey thought with evident satisfaction. *The report from Phoenix should come through on fax soon.*

The phone rang.

"Hello, FBI," Harvey intoned.

"Yeah, Phoenix here, Harv. The guy who claims he sold the van says the man's name is James Cramer—that he had an Oregon license. 'Ya mean he hasn't changed the title yet?' the guy asks. I think it's just the plates that were sold, Harv. I saw remnants of a van on this guy's lot. Probably not enough to prove anything—but I think it was a plate switch."

"Mmm-hm," Harvey nodded. "Might be right. I'm going

to run that name here in Oregon and see what I come up with—but it looks like we at least have his a.k.a. now. Anything else?"

"Yeah, we bounced this stuff off of Kansas, and they may have a lead. The name seems to have appeared in some little burg. There was mail to a farm under that name—to a farm where no one besides the owners had received mail in years. They say they'll fax you anything they get."

"Sounds good."

The two exchanged a few more bits of information and hung up.

I think our man is about to make a move, he thought, *and I wouldn't be surprised if his wife came into the picture soon.*

He picked up the receiver again and dialed Portland. "Tom Myers, please. This is Moskowitz." After an interminable wait, a voice buzzed from the other end. "I've got new stuff on Baby Kelly, and I think it warrants increased surveillance of Daniella Crabb."

The voice buzzed again—buzzed for a while.

"But, Tom—" he began, but he restrained further comment. "OK," he said and hung up.

Typical bureaucratic bullroar, he thought to himself. *Didn't even hear the evidence and the decision is made. That's the way to snatch defeat from the jaws of victory.*

Later that night after the office was closed, the fax began working. The Kansas report rolled out, indicating that the farm couple claimed to have hired a young man—Jim Cramer—and put him to work repairing some of their machines. A search of his former room revealed little except a Christian magazine with an ad for a Chicago-based ministry circled repeatedly. "Try this American Jesus Freaks place," the conclusion advised. "We've alerted Chicago—they'll wait for your word."

It was Friday night, and Harvey would not return from camping at Green Lakes in the Sisters' Mountains until Monday. The trip with his wife had been planned for too long for him to cancel it.

•

Daniella answered the knock on her door and was surprised to see Alvin Toley—it was still the middle of the day.

Toley started right in. "I don't know what it means, Daniella, but someone who saw you on the Tinnamen show has sent me a significant contribution to your cause. He wants to remain anonymous—a highly placed executive."

"What does 'significant' mean?" she asked.

When he named the figure, she sat down.

"Usually God has provided just what we need, just when we need it—and not a whole lot more. I don't know if this means we have one huge expense ahead soon or that this is going to be a real long haul," Toley remarked.

"Rather frightening," Daniella added when she caught her breath.

They both gave thanks to God and reaffirmed their trust in His invisible plan.

•

Victor smiled and grasped his toes. A gurgle reached his lips. "How about that, little? Only seven and a half months old and already grabbing your toes," Jason said. The mention of seven and a half months touched a sensitive spot in his mind—Daniella was seven and a half months pregnant with little whosit.

Ruff walked in buttoning his shirt. "I've been assigned to the paint crew for Monday, but I can take you to O'Hare Airport first thing if you don't mind hanging out there until your plane leaves."

"That's OK with me, Ruff," Jason replied. "The sooner I get moving, the better."

"Let me be candid with you, Jim," Ruff said squatting down beside Jason and the self-absorbed little baby. "The elders and I all think you are on the run from something— probably the law—but we really felt a restraint from the Lord as we prayed about whether to cough you up. I wish you would tell us more about your situation—be a bit more transparent."

Jason looked at Ruff and then at Victor. "Scripture tells us that there is a time to keep one's own counsel. I wish I could say more too, but this is complicated enough without throwing AJF into the mix."

"All right," Ruff said rising to his feet. "Time for church anyway. Let's get going."

Ruff and his wife Lisa went down the corridor toward the auditorium that AJF used for their church services. Jason mounted Victor on his hip and followed while trying to shoulder the diaper bag.

The service itself was refreshing. Jason had not been able to attend church regularly since southern California months ago. Ruff looked meaningfully at Jason as the preacher, a guest speaker from out of town, recounted the "flight to Egypt" of Mary, Joseph, and the child Jesus. "Sometimes," the speaker said, "it is necessary to flee persecution in one city and move to the next as Jesus said."

•

Very early Monday, Harvey Moskowitz piloted his compact Chevrolet into the parking garage, left the vehicle carrying his *New York Times*, and headed for his office. The office itself was dark and chilly, but Harvey did not adjust the thermostat or turn on the main lights. Instead, he flicked on the small desk lamp. As he did, his eye caught the small bundle of paper lying in the "out" tray near the fax machine. Normally, he made it a point to read the *Times* before doing anything else during his early-morning vigils, but the tension from last week's close encounter with Jason Crabb, a.k.a. James Cramer, propelled him to the silent machine. Another light stood by the machine, and Harvey switched it on.

He scanned the papers. There was a copy of a computer printout from the Oregon Motor Vehicles Department identifying a James Cramer of Turner, Oregon, just south of Salem, as the owner of a van that fit the description given by the Phoenix boys. *Looks like they were right about the plate switch,* Harvey thought. *There is a year's difference between the Oregon registration and the one from Arizona.*

Harvey turned to the next page. The report from the Kansas Bureau started there and continued for three pages. As he read, he slowly walked the three paces back to his desk.

"Bingo," he said suddenly into the empty office. He reached for the phone and punched in the number for Chicago's main Bureau office.

With the phone receiver gripped between his shoulder and ear, he continued to read the remainder of the fax message while the connection buzzed on the other end.

"Could you get me Jim Johnston? This is Harvey Moskowitz in Salem, Oregon." Johnston was an old friend of Harvey's who had even worked out of the Oregon office for a year before receiving the appointment to assistant special agent in charge in the Windy City.

"Hey, buddy," the voice from Chicago came through. "How's the fishing these days?"

"No fishing yet this year—out of season," Harvey responded, "but me and the wife just got back from camping at Green Lakes last night."

"Green Lakes? Don't tell me about it. That place is something else. Remember that time we hiked up there and fished for a week? Man, what a beautiful place. Winter camping! Wow! Did you rent horses to go up?"

"Yeah," Harvey responded.

"Well, I suppose you called on business, huh, Harv?"

"True. I got a real good nibble from a special fish, Jim. You heard about the Baby Kelly kidnapping?"

"I've seen the stuff that goes by—you know how it is. Is that your case?"

"Yeah, I've already fed the fax to you on what I have, but can you get a global search of passenger lists in and out of Chicago for this guy's a.k.a. or for a man and baby traveling alone together?"

Jim gave a low whistle. "That's a pretty large order. How big a priority is this guy?"

"He's big—for me."

"So what you're saying is that the Bureau has back-burnered the case, but you are hot to trot, right?"

"Something like that. Could you also send a couple of guys to check out this American Jesus Freaks place? It is kind of a leftover '60s commune for religious hippies. I have some info that says he might have gone there."

"You sure keep the requests coming, don't you, Harv? I'm sure I can send a couple of guys to that Jesus Freaks place. I know where it is. But I'm not sure I can get authorization for the global search. I'll do my best, OK?"

"Thanks, Jim."

•

Jason was already at the airport after abandoning the van in a part of Chicago where it was sure to be picked clean by the asphalt buzzards within a few hours. He was seated with Victor in the concourse, waiting for the boarding call as FBI agents rolled up to the headquarters of the American Jesus Freaks. A group of people stood outside the AJF doors. They were waiting for the free breakfast served by the ministry.

"Excuse me, sir." One of the agents stopped a man at the edge of the crowd.

"*Que?*"

The agent flipped out his badge, and fear crossed the man's broad, dark face.

"Green card, green card," the man said rolling the *r*'s. He quickly began to dig through his pockets.

"No, no," said the agent. "No green card." He held up a picture of Jason Crabb and asked, "Have you seen this man—Jason Crabb—James Cramer—do you know if he lives here?"

The man was visibly less fearful but answered, "*Que? No Inglais, no Inglais.*"

The agent shook his head and went to the next man. His partner was interrogating others in the group, but he also appeared to be having language difficulties. Some in the crowd were not even coherent.

"These are the wrong people to be talking to," he said to his partner. "Let's go inside."

They pressed their way through the glass doors and selected the hallway to the right rather than the stairs. A small woman in khaki pants and a bulky red sweater descended the stairway and walked purposefully past the two men.

The first agent reached out to touch her shoulder. "Excuse me," he said.

She stopped suddenly, smiled, and asked, "Can I help you?"

"Yes," the agent responded, "could you tell me who is in charge here?"

"Well, Jesus, of course," she replied without a hint of sarcasm.

Oh boy, this looks like a long interview, he thought. "But there must be some human leadership here, isn't there?" he asked, desperately hoping the answer was yes.

"Actually, there is," she answered. "Just follow me. I'll take you to some of the ones who aren't on work detail today."

She strode off without ever looking to see if they were behind. They passed several doors, turned down two other hallways, and began to ascend a set of stairs. "You guys cops?" she called back. "You look like cops. Prob'ly feds, judging by the clothes." She didn't wait for an answer. "I used to deal drugs until I met Jesus, and I used to see you guys all the time."

The two agents looked at one another as they mounted the platform at the top of the stairs. The first agent shrugged.

"This is as far as I go," their guide said indicating a doorway. "All you have to do is go down to that door at the end of the hall, and there will be someone who can help you, OK?"

The agents nodded. "Thank you," said the first.

The two stepped inside the office. At a desk covered with books and papers sat a man of approximately thirty years. His hair was spiked out in varying colors that made him resemble a vision of the Statue of Liberty on drugs. His feet were planted on the desk—or more accurately, on some books on the desk. A Bible was in the man's lap, and he was intent on reading. He raised his hand toward the agents as if to ask for another moment.

When he finished, he closed the book, and looked up. "Sorry about that. I was almost at the end of the chapter. Can I help you with something?"

"Are you in charge?" the first agent asked tentatively.

"Naw, Jesus is, but for your purposes, I am one of the elders at AJF. My name's Terry. What can I do for you?"

"We're from the FBI," said the first, displaying his ID.

"No surprises there," Terry said. "Knew it when you came in the door, that you weren't local cops. Do you guys all buy your ties from the same place?"

The agent ignored the remark. "I'm Agent Foley—this is Agent Tanzer. We're looking for this man," he said handing Terry the picture. "His name is Jason Crabb, but he goes by James Cramer. He has a baby boy with him. We have information that leads us to believe he may have come here."

"Hm-m-m. Let me see," Terry said as he carefully looked at the picture. "What's he wanted for?"

"A kidnapping in Oregon," the second agent replied before the first could stonewall.

"Wow, heavy stuff," Terry replied with a note of concern in his voice. "Gosh, we have a lot of people who live here that I hardly know—there are several hundred ministry people here, you know—but the people who stay for a night or even a week, well, I just couldn't say. Our man Ruff kind of oversees that ministry and he's on a . . . " Terry swung his chair around. "Let's see what the schedule on the wall says. Here—yes, he's on a roofing job this morning, and if there's time, a painting job this afternoon. Maybe he could call you as soon as he gets back—that all right?"

The first agent hesitated, then answered, "I'll leave that picture with you, and if you would give us the addresses of the jobs, we'll try to catch up with him. If we don't, please have him give us a call as soon as possible at this number." He handed Terry a card. "My home number is on there if I'm no longer in the office. It is very important."

"Well, kidnapping! I'm sure it is important," Terry responded. "I'll catch Ruff as soon as he arrives. Here are those addresses."

The agents thanked the spiky-haired man and departed in search of the elusive Ruff.

By noon, James and Victor Cramer were on a 727 jet bound for Washington, DC.

16

Michael McAuliff, the Irish ambassador, pushed back his white hair with his hands and wished for the thousandth time that he could rid himself of his second chin—not to mention a few pounds elsewhere. The press would be waiting for him in the conference room for a rather routine announcement, and he cringed inwardly at the thought of that chin prominently featured in the next edition of the *Washington Post*.

Two dozen press people crowded the ornate conference room, languidly awaiting the official comments on the new proposal by Northern Ireland for yet another summit to reach an accord in that divided country.

Neil Pittmon—veteran reporter and photographer in Beirut, El Salvador, Kampuchea, and a dozen other world hot spots—had been sentenced by an angry chief to "this routine tripe," in Neil's words. *Sure, there's plenty going on in DC*, he thought, but I could write the whole predictable story from the release if I didn't have to get fresh photos.

Neil hung toward the back of the room and waited. Glancing at his watch, he noted that the ambassador was already fifteen minutes late. *Typical. Probably checking his make-up.*

•

Jason and Victor had arrived in Washington's Dulles Airport shortly after three o'clock. The minimum baggage was almost too much for Jason to carry to the cab while balancing Victor on his hip. Victor was now having a wonderful time drooling and going "br-r-r-r" with his lips pursed. Bubbles of spittle ran down his chin, and he squealed often. The flight, however, had been hard on the little guy—the altitude had created havoc with his ears.

"Take me to the P Street Beach," Jason instructed the cabbie. He noted the yellow coating inside the cab and said, "The baby has breathing problems; could I ask you not to smoke on the trip?"

"Sure thing," the cabbie replied.

Upon being dropped off, Jason flipped the cabbie a good tip and then headed toward the sandy bottom next to Rock Creek. He stopped at a bench to change Victor's diaper. "No time for formalities now, little," he explained.

Jason took time to check the city map again.

Shouldering his burdens, Jason headed toward Sheridan Circle, the circular drive at the center of many of the embassy addresses. When he reached the street, he stood near the bronze statue and looked around at the ornate buildings—a hodgepodge of styles glued together. He could see the Rumanian embassy with its large clothesline-like eavesdropping antenna. Joined to it was the Irish embassy. On the walk before it stood a handful of picketers. Jason could not read the signs, but the familiar American Abortion Action Group logo was plain on several of them.

Jason shook his head. "The last hard-core baby-killers supporting Dr. Jones, I guess," he said aloud.

As he crossed the street, he saw the elegant ironwork over the entry beyond the short circular drive. Above the door, like a beacon, was a polished, brilliant green oval bearing a simple but cogent graphic design of a harp.

Clutching Victor, Jason stepped beneath it.

•

Neil Pittmon stood in back of the room and focused his camera on the podium microphone. He blessed the day when the zoom lens had been invented because of the many advantages of a little distance from the action—especially the kind of action he often encountered.

McAuliff had just entered the room and begun to shuffle a few papers when an aide appeared at the door and scurried to the ambassador's side. Cupping a hand, he whispered into the man's ear.

Through the lens, Neil watched McAuliff's eyes dilate with evident interest in the whispered message. Neil smelled something that had the distinct tang of "story" and artfully excused himself. The aide profusely apologized to the remaining pressmen for an "unavoidable" delay as McAuliff exited.

Pittmon became part of the wall as he had learned in combat zones while he watched McAuliff come into the corridor and head straight for the foyer where a small clutch of people stood. The reporter made his way toward the head of the hallway, taking care not to attract notice.

Pittmon's uncanny hearing had gotten him out of many a tight spot—and into many a great story. His ears picked up a woman telling McAuliff, " . . . says he wants political asylum—from the United States."

Pittmon was silently praying to the god of journalists that the people in the group would pull back so he could shoot a picture of this seeker of asylum, but his prayers fell flat.

Continuing to listen, Neil overheard a man's voice saying, "Your country's official policy protects life, sir, and there was no other hope for me—or for Victor—but to flee the U.S. Victor here is facing death, and I face a long imprisonment for trying to save him. Perhaps you have heard of our case. A friend advised me that the U.N. has criteria for refugee status and that my situation would be in accordance with . . ."

"The 1951 Convention and the 1967 Protocol," McAuliff supplied the citation. "Yes. Yes, indeed, Mr., ah, Mr. . . ."

"Crabb," Jason said.

"Yes, Mr. Crabb. They may indeed apply, but that will require further study."

Inwardly, McAuliff grinned. A plan was formulating in his mind. "Mr. Crabb, tell me, are you now in fear for your life?"

As he asked this question, the group opened, and Jason was clearly visible in Pittmon's viewfinder. Jason held Victor, who was squirming, though quiet. "No, but I am in fear for Victor's life."

Crabb. Neil searched his memory. *Crabb—the kidnapper*! Neil snapped off three shots, praying that his camera noise would not break into the cozy scene. He then disappeared and went back to the conference room.

Jason was still speaking. "In fact, I think the FBI is on my trail."

"The other question is equally important: Have you spoken to the press?"

"No."

"Good," McAuliff answered. "We will grant temporary asylum while we research this and hope we can make it public when we are ready to answer questions more knowledgeably." The ambassador turned to the woman beside him. "Take him to my office. Make him—and Victor—comfortable." He reached out and touched the baby's face. "Death, is it now?" he said, and headed back to the conference room.

Soon the press conference was over, and the last of the reporters were oozing out of the room. As McAuliff stepped out into the hall he heard the voice of Neil Pittmon. "Mr. Ambassador? May I have a word with you?"

17

"BABY KELLY KIDNAPPER SEEKS ASYLUM," read the headline above the photo of Jason holding Victor. Neil Pittmon grinned with satisfaction at the front page byline and photo credit.

All of Washington was buzzing. The wire services had just gotten the item and were busily sending the story around the world. The networks scrambled to get as much information as possible on this turn of events—but the Irish embassy was tight-lipped. A news conference would be announced "as soon as the situation could be carefully studied in the light of the U.N. Human Rights Declarations and information from the High Commission for Refugees in Geneva, Switzerland."

"We've got the American press on a string this time," chortled Ambassador McAuliff. "This time they can only come to us, and we can turn the tables on their long harangue over that abortionist Jones."

McAuliff leaned back in his chair and said to the empty office, "Let's let the press hang out without a word for a few days. Let the public wonder what's going on."

•

In Salem, Oregon, however, a small group of people knew of the situation even before Neil Pittmon's scoop hit the streets. Jason had phoned Daniella. She told the kids what was happening and led them in a prayer of thanks even before she called Alvin Toley. Toley's whoop could be heard a considerable distance from Daniella's receiver—and it was also relayed to Harvey Moskowitz from the intermittent telephone tap on the Crabb household.

"Well, I'll be," Moskowitz said shaking his head and acknowledging to himself that Jason's move had been "pretty slick."

•

Official Washington had been stunned into inaction by the first reports. But now Pat and Robert Kelly's connections were calling. Euthanasia lobbying groups chimed in that this "criminal" must be brought to justice. Even the American Abortion Action Group, which had been picketing over the Irish abortionist Dr. Jones, joined the cry for the government to assert its authority to protect "the right to privacy" in medical decisions. AAAG president Betsy Winkler cut short a speaking tour to fly to Washington where she told the press, "This may be the most important front of the right-to-privacy battle at this moment. Privacy must not only include abortion, but the right of parents to choose medical treatment for their children."

Dominic Stanford from Americans for Medical Choice was already in town where his group was headquartered and stood arm-in-arm with the Ms. Winkler. After her comments, Stanford added, "The American principle of choice is what is under attack here. People like Jason Crabb are as unamerican as King George III—they would make all Americans' choices *for* them. Our government must insist that Crabb and the child be turned over."

A growing crowd outside the Irish embassy chanted for McAuliff to surrender Jason. Police soon had the area cordoned off with yellow police-line tape, and protesters were moved to Sheridan Circle across the street.

With the chants a dim sound in the background, McAuliff sat serenely inside his office waiting for Jason to arrive. He rose as Jason came through the door bearing Victor in his arms. "Good day to you, Mr. Crabb—and to you, Victor. Please, have a seat."

McAuliff lowered himself into his chair. "Mr. Crabb," he began, "I want you to know that even though you have only been here three days, the decision has already been made to grant your request for asylum."

Jason's eyes opened wide in surprise.

"Allow me to explain, Mr. Crabb. The decision was made the day you arrived. All of the talk about 'studying the matter' is a convenience to clear certain matters of protocol." McAuliff added in his mind, *And to sweat the American press.* "Certainly you must have guessed that your government—or should I say your former government—has been making requests—if they can be called that. The FBI has insisted on your extradition, as it were, from sovereign Irish territory. There are other formalities to follow while this 'study' continues—none of which will have the least effect on our decision. I only ask that you keep this knowledge to yourself—even your wife cannot be told. This 'study' should be over, hmm, probably by next Wednesday. Meanwhile, there will be increasing government surveillance aimed at keeping you here as well as an increasing crowd of protesters out in the park. The proper handling of this situation will be very delicate, Mr. Crabb. It is like a great game of chess—each trying to anticipate the strategies of the other and developing gambits many moves ahead. Yours was an excellent opening move for an exciting game, but there are yet many moves before a checkmate. Can you see that?"

"Sure," Jason replied, placing the squirming Victor on the expensive carpet and secretly hoping that he would not "urp" on it. "All this diplomacy stuff is your racket, Mr. McAuliff. I'll leave it entirely in your hands."

"Splendid," McAuliff said, smiling as he mentally planned the announcement of the Irish people's deep concern for life—and especially the lives of little babies—with a backdrop of a huge death-demanding crowd.

•

Harvey Moskowitz looked a little ragged around the edges. He had had little sleep since he first heard of the whereabouts of his quarry—but he hardly noticed the sleeplessness. "We need 'round the clock surveillance on Daniella Crabb and family," he barked to his agents and handed them a schedule. "No need to be cagy—just ride herd on that crew. If there is a time when we can expect a move, it will be now."

Moskowitz turned on his heel and dialed the Portland office. "Give me Tom Myers. This is Harvey Moskowitz."

An hour later, Harvey was still trying to convince Myers to put him on special assignment to spearhead the group in Washington, DC. "Of course, we don't know which way this will go, Tom. That's exactly why you need me there. I'm the one who has the best handle on this guy. The boys here can keep an eye on his family. You know me, Tom. I'm not just trying to wheedle a trip across the country out of the Bureau—I'm genuinely interested in resolving this case."

"OK, OK," Myers finally answered. "I'll talk to the SAC about it."

An hour later, Harvey was heading home to pack. But before he strode out the door, he left detailed instructions for the watch over Daniella. "I don't want to hear of any screw-ups," he warned. "These people have more going for them than it appears."

•

Within twenty-four hours of Harvey Moskowitz's departure, the surveillance team slipped into a routine. It wasn't that they were not alert. Rather it was an assumption that had crept into their thinking that Daniella and company were entirely predictable. Harvey would have seen it in their attitude as readily as a fluorescent name badge, and he would have pounced on it instantly.

All of the men had, at one time or another, been part of the partial surveillance on the Crabb crew, and all could see how predictable they were. Only Harvey could not see it, they thought.

A sturdy-looking agent drove his unadorned Ford up across from the Crabb house. It was nearly 5 a.m. on a cool Sunday morning. The agent in the other car walked back and leaned into the Ford's window. "Changing of the guard, huh?"

"Yeah," replied the new arrival. "They'll be going to church as usual, then home and probably have some guests over for dinner. Sunday's the easiest to watch this bunch."

The other yawned and glanced at his watch. "Punch out

time," he said. "Have a nice day," he added with a sarcastic grin.

The new man said in mock anger, "Hey, don't tell me what kind of day to have."

The hours passed slowly. Daniella was soon loading her clan into the car and waddling around to the driver's door where she carefully maneuvered her large stomach behind the steering wheel. By now she had adjusted the seat so far back that she would have difficulty reaching the pedals.

The agent ran his fingers through his blond hair and then started the motor on the Ford as soon as Daniella started hers. *It's not like it is a secret*, he thought as he wheeled the vehicle in behind Daniella's car at the stop sign at the corner.

Daniella turned right onto Broadway and made the short jaunt to the old, clapboard-sided church. The Fellowship Hall was a newer extension of the building, and Daniella herded her crew into the side entrance of the stucco structure.

The agent looked at his watch. *It's 10:00 now, and it will be about 12:30 when they let out. That should give me some time to read the paper.* He reached to the passenger side, slid a copy of the Sunday *Oregonian* into his lap, and began to rifle through it.

Regularly glancing up and at his watch, the agent managed to get through the points of interest in the entire paper before the doors to the church swung open and crowds issued forth. Several times the agent noted the blue dress of Daniella Crabb in the crowd. A knot of people seemed to be talking to her and escorting her to her car. *Probably a lot of questions about Jason's little trick*, the agent thought to himself.

He saw her and the children loaded into the car, and he followed as she pulled out of the lot, drove home, and emptied the vehicle into the side door of the modest home where they lived.

Well, all we need to know is if they will have dinner guests this week, he thought.

•

What the agent failed to see was the small group leaving by the church's side entrance and boarding a tan station wagon. The wagon left the parking lot on a side street, went around the block, circuitously reached Broadway, and turned south toward the Salem Municipal Airport at McNary Field. Waiting for the wagon was a Lear 35 and a pilot.

Daniella, in a red and black knit dress, emerged from the vehicle with the children. Their driver, a nameless friend of Alvin Toley's, stepped from behind the wheel and walked over to the pilot and handed him a cashier's check for his services. The pilot nodded and boarded the plane. Looking back, he asked, "You sure this pregnant lady can handle the flight?"

"You want a doctor's slip maybe?" Alvin's friend asked.

The pilot shrugged.

Daniella's escort grinned widely and then climbed into the sleek eight-passenger Lear jet. Daniella helped each child into the aircraft and held her escort's hand as she stepped aboard. After she had secured the seat belts of all the children, both adults sat toward the rear. The unnamed man opened a briefcase. "I have passports and new identification for all of you. The children's first names are the same, but you are now Lisa Caldwell. Here are tickets to your destination." He handed the stack of documents to Daniella. "When we get to J.F.K. Airport, we drop you off and head straight out—you'll be on your own. You'll find we supplied you with travelers' cheques enough to keep you for a while—at least until you are able to execute the plan, OK?"

Daniella nodded. As the Lear 35 taxied out toward the runway, a cloud darkened the February sky. A wind-driven mist hit the small porthole window on Daniella's right. *Lord, give us protection from all our enemies.*

18

It was like a scene from a nightmare. Harvey Moskowitz stood atop a platform on an FBI van and surveyed the crowds. Capitol police had closed off the circle and confined demonstrators to an area across the street from the embassy. People filled the circular park and the street behind, threatening to cork all the avenues that spoked into Sheridan Circle.

Turning to the Irish embassy, Harvey noted the open windows on the third story where Ambassador McAuliff had said he would announce his decision on Crabb and the baby (now called Victor). "The conclusion is foregone," Harvey thought aloud.

A local agent lowered his field glasses. "Hmm?"

"Nothing," responded Harvey.

Harvey's men worked with the DC police checking ID and allowing legitimate press to fill the embassy's circular drive and the street before it. His own van was located in front of the Greek embassy.

The Irish had placed PA speakers on the ironwork around the third-floor windows, and the brilliant green of their national flag fluttered slowly and boldly from the standard on the second balcony.

"Bring the baby out, bring the baby out!" came the current chant from the crowds. Intermittently it changed to, "Crabb is a kidnapper; arrest him, arrest him!"

Harvey had operatives circulating through the mass of people in search of potentially violent ones. A sky watch scanned local roofs.

The chants grew louder and angrier as the ten o'clock deadline came and went. The police grew noticeably tense—especially those who stood shoulder to shoulder in the front line.

Suddenly, a few stanzas of the Irish national anthem sounded from the speakers. The crowds settled to a murmur, and McAuliff stepped up to the open window holding a microphone.

This guy really knows how to play it, Harvey thought with a hint of admiration.

"Ladies and gentlemen, members of the press, allow me to introduce Mr. Jason Crabb and Victor," McAuliff said with an air of gravity.

The two appeared at the window beside McAuliff. Harvey quickly scanned the neighboring rooftops and the crowds.

The crowds erupted, screaming the chant, "Arrest him, arrest him, arrest him."

Harvey noted McAuliff calmly holding his hand out as though his palm could hold back the crashing sea of verbal hatred. The scene brought to Harvey's mind another event from centuries past—Pontius Pilate playing to the crowds chanting, "Crucify Him, crucify Him." *Only this time Pilate makes the right decision and dumps on the crowd*, he thought.

But the words *right decision* startled Harvey's conscious mind. He looked at the thought, shelved it for future consideration, and returned to his careful surveillance. Finally, the crowd's din died, and McAuliff continued.

"I wish to introduce Mr. Jason Crabb and his adopted son, Victor, as Irish citizens."

Two seconds of stunned silence followed; then a clamor filled the air. Hooting, screaming radical leftists strained against the police line, and police quickly pulled their batons. The crowd eased back, with the exception of a handful of people wearing "Pro-choice" shirts. These were stopped, cuffed, and efficiently lugged away to a waiting paddy wagon.

Harvey was not just hearing McAuliff's words, however; he was analyzing them. *What of Crabb's family?* he wondered pointedly.

•

The massive wheels of the 747 sent out plumes of smoke as they touched the tarmac at the Dublin, Ireland, airport. The craft wheeled ponderously to the terminal, shuddered to a stop, and disgorged its human cargo. At the end of this stream came a dark-haired pregnant woman with a small herd of children.

Daniella and her brood entered Customs and presented the pile of falsified passports.

"Come over here, Nicole," she called after the wandering three-year-old.

An Irish voice asked Daniella a few cursory questions and passed the group through.

"The office of the Prime Minister—the Taoiseach,"

Daniella said to the hack driver as she loaded the children aboard and he filled the trunk.

"Won't you be wantin' to go to your hotel first, ma'am?" the driver asked as he pulled away from the loading zone.

"No. Our first business is with the Taoiseach," Daniella responded.

"All right, ma'am. It just seemed a lot of baggage to be takin' into a government office, is all."

"It's all right, sir," Daniella answered—and she said no more.

Daniella paid scant attention as they drove past the city's ancient stone buildings. She was in prayer for the upcoming challenge. The cabbie discharged his load and drove off. The children carried what luggage they could and followed their mother into the ornate office. They looked like refugees beside the opulence of the anteroom.

"May I help you?" asked the red-haired receptionist.

"I'm Daniella Crabb, and I'm here to personally plead on behalf of my husband, Jason Crabb, who has taken refuge in your embassy in Washington, DC. May I see the Taoiseach, please?"

The receptionist's mouth went slack as her eyes widened. "Ah . . . ah, let me see what can be done," she said and suddenly ducked toward her intercom.

Shortly, a well-dressed brunette appeared from behind the massive doors. "You say your name is Crabb—*Mrs.* Crabb?"

"Yes—"

"Well then, something must be done—quickly. You haven't spoken to anyone, have you?—the press?" she asked with an edge of anxiety in her voice.

"No—" Daniella began again.

"Well then—good! Follow me. Just leave your bags. They will be collected later."

The brunette appeared speedy even when she walked slowly enough for Daniella's ponderous waddle. "The Taoiseach has not been as supportive as our Washington ambassador has of your husband's claim for relief," she confided to Daniella as they walked down the hall.

Daniella smiled and nodded.

"I just don't know how he'll respond to this new development. This is most irregular—I'm sure you know, Mrs. Crabb."

Again, Daniella smiled and nodded.

"Well then—you may all wait in this room. I will see that the Taoiseach is informed of your presence."

With that, the woman disappeared through the door back to the hall.

●

Harvey's urgent call to the Salem office came as soon as the first agent walked through the door in the morning. "Go have someone knock on the door and find out close-up if Crabb's wife and kids are still home," he barked.

"But we've had someone on 'em round the clock, Harv," the agent replied.

"I think you've been had. I'm willing to bet that whoever is in that house is not the Crabbs."

"OK, Harv. We'll do it," the agent answered.

He hung up the phone and headed for his vehicle.

●

U.S. State Department functionary Donald Billings was a nondescript, drab individual with little ambition. It was, therefore, meet that he was selected to carry out the thankless task of delivering the ultimatum to the Irish ambassador. The eventual press conference would be left to more colorful figures.

The office spooks and politicos had anticipated Ambassador McAuliff's decision, so the response had already been prepared. Billings was dispatched as soon as the ambassador went public.

The excitement of the provocative announcement was over, but demonstrators still remained around the embassy. Billings's credentials let him pass easily through police—police used to seeing government ID flashed. But Billings merely showed, rather than flashed, his credentials.

The missive Billings carried was signed by very high-powered people, but the message was simple. Translated into common tongue, it said, "We want Crabb and the baby. We will not violate your sovereignty, but we will not allow them to leave the embassy."

The siege was on.

●

Jason entered the ambassador's office with some hesitation. The place still overawed him.

"Ah, Mr. Crabb," said McAuliff. "Come in, come in. I have good news. Your attorney from Oregon, Mr. Toley, informs me that he has supplied us the 'mate'—in more ways than one—to our 'check' move today. It could not be better."

"What's happened?" Jason asked.

"Someone—Mr. Toley declined to identify him—has arranged for your wife and children to be flown to Ireland to personally appeal your case to the Prime Minister and ask for asylum for the rest of your clan."

"Wha—" Jason began.

McAuliff held up his hand. "Mr. Crabb, it couldn't have been better timed if the Lord Himself had done it. You see, the Taoiseach—the Prime Minister—was not altogether in agreement with my decision to grant you asylum. He was threatening to—how do you say it—'pull the plug' on me. I merely beat him to the punch, and now your wife is delivering the second hard blow. The Taoiseach can hardly refuse your pregnant wife and children—in person—without looking awfully heartless."

"Then it's settled?" Jason asked.

Laughter shook the man's large frame. "Mr. Crabb, things are never quite over—in the words of one American philosopher—until they are over. The U.S. State Department still demands your return. The FBI still watches. Both tell us they will not let you leave this embassy—thereby crossing their sovereign territory—to go to Ireland. That, of course, remains to be seen. There are still many possible moves in this game. It is no stalemate."

There was a joyful glitter in McAuliff's eye.

•

The Taoiseach was a spindly old man with long, thinning white hair brushed straight back from the remainder of his widow's peak. He sat forward on the edge of the stuffed leather chair by the fireplace. His palms were planted firmly on his knees, and the knobby, long fingers looked like talons. His feet were wide apart and flat on the floor, and his elbows shot straight out from his shoulders. He reminded Daniella ever so much of a large gray spider.

"Ye must under-r-rstand, Mrs. Cr-r-rabb, that this whole

affair-r-r has given us a gr-r-reat deal of conster-r-rnation," he said seriously with his head slightly cocked.

"I quite understand, Mr. Prime Minister," Daniella responded. "But this has been a matter of life and death."

"That it has," the Taoiseach said gravely.

A moment of silence prevailed as both seemed to study the patterns in the carpet. Finally the Taoiseach began again. "It wouldn't be r-r-right to send ye away this late in the game, now would it? And especially with the children."

Daniella felt the child inside give a tremendous kick as if responding to the words. It seemed the interview was over—as well as Daniella's flight.

Only Jason remained dangling.

19

The *Post* headline screamed, "KIDNAPPER'S WIFE FLEES TO IRELAND, BEGS ASYLUM." The network anchorwoman—every hair in place—intoned gravely, "Today it was discovered that Daniella Crabb and her children, the family of the Baby Kelly kidnapper, have surfaced in Dublin, Ireland, and there have sought political asylum for themselves and Jason Crabb.

"Jason Crabb, the kidnapper of Baby Kelly—now widely known as Victor—has been sequestered in the Irish embassy in Washington, DC, for almost two weeks. The discovery of his family in Ireland coincides with the announcement earlier yesterday by Irish ambassador McAuliff that Crabb's request for asylum had been accepted. Only shortly afterward, the Irish Prime Minister accepted the rest of the family's appeal for asylum as well.

"U.S. authorities are insisting that the Irish government surrender Jason Crabb and Victor, but many in the administration express reservations in private. Both pro-life and pro-choice groups have mounted heavy pressure campaigns to release or arrest the Oregon mechanic. Inside sources say the calls and letters to the White House are running about evenly split on the issue. Pro-life groups claim that the vast majority of people favor Crabb and that reports of pro-choice strength are distorted.

"Meanwhile, daily vigils outside the embassy continue with pro-choice and death-with-dignity groups in strongest evidence. Robert and Pat Kelly, the parents of the kidnapped child, have joined the daily demonstrations."

Rumors abounded—as they always do in Washington—that secret negotiations were taking place between the White House and Ambassador McAuliff on the delicate matter.

Harvey Moskowitz received mixed signals. As agent-in-charge of this operation, he heard about every squeaky wheel that wanted grease for its side of the issue. But official word still called for the capture of Jason Crabb and the recovery of Victor.

Harvey had had time to reflect further on the thought he had shelved on the day of the announcement. He concluded that McAuliff had indeed done the "right thing." Still, Harvey was was FBI—and as FBI, he would carry the case out accordingly. Harvey's assigned men kept up constant surveillance outside the Irish embassy. Not willing to strap the others with all the dirty work, he assigned himself to many of the night watches.

One night, about a week after the announcement by McAuliff, the assistant special agent-in-charge for Washington, DC, pulled his car up behind Harvey's parked vehicle. The older man invited himself inside and parked his short, heavy frame on the passenger side of the seat.

"How does it look, Harv?" he asked.

"Looks like a long haul—and possibly a lost cause," Harvey replied bluntly.

When Harvey had first emerged from training, he had

been assigned to Cincinnati where this man had been a senior agent. They had worked together on and off for Harvey's first ten years with the Bureau. They had never been close, but they had gotten to know one another fairly well.

"Why don't you fill me in on this—from the beginning— and give me your honest impressions. Just between us, OK?" the older man said.

Harvey was cautious. He entirely distrusted the whole "openness" psychobabble movement and its government agency equivalent. He knew how political games ran rampant in the Bureau—especially in DC.

He gave the ASAC a complete briefing on the case, including a personal profile of Jason Crabb.

"I have no doubt the man is sincere and of good character. But I think the situation got deeper than he had originally planned. Still he had the moxie to carry it through—legal risks and all. In that sense, he's no more dangerous than my plumber. But allowed to continue, this kind of thing could get out of hand—it could be a legal disaster if he inspires others. I think our holing him up here brings more attention to the—shall I say, 'rightness' of his cause and may encourage others to do the same."

After the pause, Harvey added, "It also makes us look like powerful persecutors hounding an ordinary guy and a baby—not good for the image."

The ASAC drew a breath and said, "That's the feeling I'm getting from a lot of the guys." But the ASAC conveniently omitted saying just who any of the "guys" were. Harvey had the savvy not to ask—he was waiting for the other shoe to drop.

The ASAC continued, "Yeah, they say it might be almost worth it to be rid of the both of them—let him, as it were, slip through our fingers. Of course, no one could *officially* do it in the present climate—would really catch it for that—but it could *just happen*, you know. And it would get the high-muck-de-mucks off the hook."

"Be bad for whoever was on watch though," Harvey said, as if casting a fishing line in search of a bite.

"True," the ASAC replied. "'Specially if he were some young buck with big-time career goals. He'd likely be banished to some remote outpost like Salem, Oregon, or something."

"Prob'ly," Harvey commented.

The two sat quietly in the car for several more minutes. "Pretty quiet around here this time of night, I mean, no one paying attention to the embassy like they are during the day, huh? Not even much in the way of traffic."

"That's right," answered Harvey. He did not need the whole of Embassy Row to fall in on him to understand the ASAC's words. Harvey was well aware of the Washington game. "By the way, let me give you a copy of my schedule so you know when I'm working," Harvey added as he quickly wrote down the information.

"Good idea. Well, thanks for the rundown on the case. It helps me put the whole thing in better perspective. Have a good night, Harv."

"Any time," Harvey nodded. "G'night."

•

"But the FBI car is still there," Jason whispered as though the silhouetted agent could hear his words through the embassy's stone facade.

"Don't worry, Mr. Crabb," the ambassador assured Jason as he opened the front door. Outside stood an idling limousine with its rear door flung wide. "Your baggage is inside—I'll accompany you to the airport to see you off."

"But—"

"No time for 'buts,' Mr. Crabb. It is time to seal this gambit and announce our checkmate."

Jason hefted the chunky little Victor and walked out the door. A cold March wind hit Victor in the face, and he let out a yowl that would seem to Jason to wake the very world of Washington. But the hawk-faced man behind the wheel of the obviously "unmarked" car did not stir.

They all climbed into the elongated Cadillac, and it quietly rolled out to the street and began a direct route to the airport. "Your citizenship papers and official recognition of adoption for Victor will be given you once aboard the Taoiseach's personal transport plane—he sent it over for you. It is the poor Irish version of *Air Force One*."

Jason hardly knew what to say, so he said nothing.

It was only when Jason was on the plane and it took to the air that the reality of his adventure finally fully settled in his mind. He reviewed the immense Providential care he had witnessed throughout the entire eight-and-one-half-month exodus. And now this. A new life in the Old World. *How very like God,* he thought, *to work out such an exploit—and all without any credit to anyone but Him.*

He reached for his Bible as a verse came to his mind, Isaiah 42:16. It read, "I will lead the blind by ways they have not known, along unfamiliar paths I will guide them; I will turn the darkness into light before them and make the rough places smooth. These are the things I will do; I will not forsake them."

Tears came to Jason's eyes as he lifted silent praise to God and asked, "But why me, Lord?"

The answer was instantaneous as the Spirit brought the

proverb to mind, "Trust in the Lord with all your heart and
lean not on your own understanding; in all your ways
acknowledge him, and he will make your paths straight."

The night sky sped by the small windows, and the sun
was rising a thousand miles away on an Emerald Isle where
a persecuted Christian once wrote, "I see His blood upon
the rose . . . "—an island that was now a new refuge for this
small clan of God's people.